Total-E-Bound Publishing books by Genella DeGrey:

Love Divine
Masterpiece
A Touch of Destiny
Sins of the Flesh

I0570649

WHISKED AWAY

GENNELLA DEGREY

Whisked Away
ISBN # 978-1-78184-561-5
©Copyright Genella deGrey 2013
Cover Art by Posh Gosh ©Copyright July 2012
Interior text design by Claire Siemaszkiewicz
Total-E-Bound Publishing

Published in 2013 by Total-E-Bound Publishing, Think Tank, Ruston Way, Lincoln, LN6 7FL, United Kingdom.

Total-E-Bound Publishing is an imprint of Total-E-Ntwined Limited.

WHISKED AWAY

Dedication

If you thought Luke and Beatrice's story had a touch of destiny to it, you will find that Rory and Virginia's story possesses that same 'touch.'

Chapter One

Fifth Avenue Hotel, New York
June 1892

Rory Hughson's temper seethed. "I know these artistic types—rakes, rogues and seducers of women, all. Tell her, Ace. Tell her she cannot go through with this nonsensical scheme."

Virginia had never seen him like this. Then again, she hadn't seen him in a dozen years or so. Oh, yes, he was still quite handsome with his full head of dark blond hair that she wanted to plunge her fingers into and smooth down his neck, but at the moment, she wouldn't get within arm's distance of that six-foot-tall broiling oven. "Beatrice, please tell your brother-in-law he is not my mother."

"Of course I'm not your mother," he snapped before Beatrice could speak. "But since she's three thousand miles away in Tombstone, someone has to rein in the wild filly."

Now he was starting to get personal, and that wouldn't do at all. "Wild filly?" Virginia spun to face the guardian of her youth. "Have I not been the very picture of respectability since I came to live with you and Luke?"

Before either Beatrice or 'Ace', as Rory called his older brother Luke, could answer, Rory voiced his opinion. "Miss Clark, you are still going to need a suitable companion."

Oh, if I could just reach him, I'd choke him like a chicken. "For your information, Mr Hughson, pastry chefs do not go about their kitchens with chaperones!"

Rory folded his arms over his chest in a blatant display of annoyance. "Ace, perhaps you should have Beatrice accompany her. It would behove you both to keep this young miss out of trouble."

A breath of air hit the back of Ginny's throat like a bubble beaten from a lump of dough. Her thoughts skittered about. She was beyond shocked that Rory would even suggest that she would attract any sort of conflict...*her*, a woman who'd just achieved something few other females of her meagre means had ever dreamed of— "Out of trouble? Why, I never—"

The twit, Rory, had the audacity to interrupt her with a condescending chuckle. "Never? I seem to recall a certain carriage ride from Tombstone to Tucson—"

"Rory." Thankfully, Luke spoke up. "I think you've shown your hand."

Beatrice Hughson glanced up at her husband from the elegant green silk brocade settee. "May Ginny and I have a moment, darling?" At his nod Beatrice rose, and with an air of grace she floated into the next room. Virginia, too irritated to follow Beatrice's lady-like example, stomped past the brothers Hughson and slammed the door behind her.

"Beatrice—"

"Please sit, Ginny."

Virginia plopped down onto the nearest chaise. Beatrice was the only person whom she allowed to call her by her childhood nickname.

Beatrice sat on the matching wing-back chair opposite her and arranged her skirts about her as if they were about to have a tea party, not discuss Virginia's controversial summer plans.

"I didn't get to tell you how lovely you looked at your commencement ceremony today," Beatrice said, still not making eye contact with her. "Your mother would have been proud, had she the means to journey across the country."

"Thank you," she said with sincerity. Virginia had kept in contact with her mother via the post, but Mrs Clark seemed content to remain out west. "It was very kind of you to travel up from Virginia. I can't tell you how happy I was to see you among the assembled." She loved Beatrice. If it hadn't been for her, she wouldn't have had the advantage of such a thorough education. She'd probably still be stuck in that hole-in-the-desert, sharing a classroom with a few miners' children of various ages. Virginia was overjoyed she'd spent her more formative years with the Hughsons. The sun hadn't set on a single day since she'd arrived when Virginia didn't thank the stars above that Beatrice and Luke had looked the other way after she'd stowed away, unchaperoned with Rory to Tucson. Well, mostly looked the other way. She understood now that a tiny indiscretion like that could ruin one's chance of...well, anything.

Beatrice folded her hands in her lap. "Now, you must admit, spending an entire summer in France with total strangers is rather an odd thing to do for a woman—a woman with legitimate social and familial connections here in the States."

Beatrice's gaze, which normally conveyed an affable, loving calmness, bored into Virginia's. It was a shame that Beatrice and Luke had never produced any children. Beatrice would have made an extraordinary mother.

Virginia gripped the arms of the chair with damp palms, the absorbent lace doilies suffering the moisture. "But Beatrice, I won the contest. They chose me, out of all the other students—how could I refuse such an honour and not label myself a coward, unfit for the culinary arts?"

"My dear, is that all you're worried about? Good Heavens, we love you for who you are, not for...for whom you cook."

Virginia remembered the many times that she and Beatrice had prepared meals for the less fortunate miners every Sunday back in Tombstone. Stone Soup Night was the sole reason Virginia had become so enamoured with cooking. "It's not that." She sighed. "Please don't think me ungrateful for everything you and Luke have done but I wish to make my own way in the world. The only acceptable approach is to prove it among strangers, not with those who already accept me."

Beatrice seemed to be absorbing this thought as Virginia continued. Now was the time to fully plead her case. "If I could actually make a living doing what I love, I wouldn't have to depend upon anyone but myself. Why, Juliet Corson, the woman who founded the New York Cooking School way back in seventy-two, kicked open this wondrous door for us. Now here we are, twenty years later and the opportunity of a lifetime stands before me in all its glory."

She waited for Beatrice to speak, but only for a moment. There was one more point she needed to make to close her argument. "Even back then, Miss Corson's intent was for unemployed working-class women to find employment expressly in the domestic arts." Virginia was loath to sound whiny. She straightened her back. "It was her dream, and it is mine, too."

"Very well."

Virginia's heart leapt and she bounced out of her seat. "Oh, thank—"

"Just a moment. Before you go packing your trunks for Paris, I wish to discuss the topic of a chaperone."

She sank back down to the chair. "I assure you, Beatrice. I do not need a chaperone."

Beatrice leant forward and placed her hand over Virginia's. "It would put my heart mightily at ease if you would take someone familiar along."

To this Virginia remained silent. She wished neither for a companion nor to lose the respect of Beatrice and Luke.

"My only regret is that I cannot attend you myself." Beatrice sat back in her chair. "My ladies' society fundraiser and tea is next month, and it wouldn't at all be the thing to cancel."

"I could never ask you to do so. Your letters informed me of how long and hard you've been working to make the tea a success."

Beatrice nodded once, then sighed. "Your mother, then? I'm sure Luke would be willing to purchase a train—"

"I cannot bring my mother with me while pursuing my profession." She hadn't meant to sound indignant, but how else should she react to such a suggestion?

A significant pause drew on, like watching water not boiling. "I'd ask Luke to accompany you, but for him to be away from the plantation for an entire summer would be—"

"Oh, Beatrice, I wouldn't hear of it."

Beatrice nodded and her shoulders relaxed some. "There is, however, one more question I must put to you before we go any further."

Curious, Virginia's brows lifted. "And that is?"

Beatrice fidgeted, but only for a moment. "Do you still have romantic ideas regarding Rory?"

* * * *

"You do understand why she is in need of a companion, don't you?"

Ace's eyebrow angled over a knowing blue eye. "It is not I you need to convince. It's the ladies in the next room."

"But surely you have some say in what Beatrice thinks."

His older brother chuckled in a rather mocking fashion.

Rory fisted his hands and placed them on his hips, resisting the urge to punch his sibling in the nose.

"You have much to learn about women—strong, intelligent, independent-minded women that is, not the simpering Southern gals who forever cling to their mama's skirts, much like the ones you likely encountered while living with Aunt Iris."

"The women down south are much more refined than up here." It was an absurd statement and he knew it. The female of the species hardly differed at all between the northern and the southern states, but Rory couldn't think about that right now—not when he hadn't convinced his brother to take charge of Ginny's pending impropriety. "Anyone with the sense of a honey bee would agree that Ginny should have a chaperone."

Ace shrugged. "So move back to Charleston. I guarantee you won't find refinement very satisfying in the bedroom."

Rory strode to the opposite end of the room. "Spare me your sordid ideals, you and my sister-in-law..." He spun on his heel. "Wait a minute, just what are you insinuating?"

Ace hooked his thumb into the watch pocket of his fancy gold and cardinal waistcoat. His cool demeanour only served to irritate Rory further. "Correct me if I'm wrong, but you were attracted to Virginia at one time, weren't you?"

"I was, we were..." Rory despised the fact that he'd sputtered. "It was a long time ago, Ace."

"I see." Ever so casually, Ace flipped open his watch for a moment, then tucked it back into the pocket. "Tell me, Rory." He adjusted his watch fob so that it hung evenly and pinned Rory with a meaningful stare. "What are your feelings towards Virginia now?"

Chapter Two

Virginia stood. "Of course I don't have romantic ideas about him." She turned and strode to the window. Had she answered too quickly? She set her hand upon the wooden window pane, trying to appear casual. "Why, he's like family." The truth was, Rory had grown into a fine man, even more handsome than when they'd first met years ago. But she was disinclined to share her feelings with Beatrice until she knew how Rory felt. At the moment it seemed Rory's intended association with her only extended to little sister. "Why, he's more like a brother to me."

"I see," came Beatrice's reply. Virginia wished with all her heart that she could read between those two words as to their real meaning.

"Come. Let us return to the sitting room. It's nearly tea time. Luke gets simply ravenous every day at this time."

Beatrice rose and Virginia followed dutifully.

The first face Virginia's gaze landed upon as they entered was Rory's. His crystalline blue eyes, although slightly darkened since his youth, were wide as if he'd been caught pilfering from the sugar bowl.

"I have none. None, whatsoever." Rory had spoken quietly, but Virginia still caught the statement he'd tossed at his brother.

What had they been discussing? Virginia told herself she shouldn't care about anything he said. She flounced past him, masking her nerves. With shaking legs she lowered herself to the window seat, and faced the window. Funny how she suddenly felt like a child in the presence of Beatrice and Luke, she hadn't been at all susceptible to emotional outbursts while at school.

A knock sounded at the door and a uniformed maid from the hotel wheeled in a tea cart. Beatrice directed the pour out, but before Luke could swallow the bite of buttered muffin he'd taken, his wife took him by the hand.

"Would you see me in the other room for a moment, dear? I may have a solution to our predicament."

Luke trailed behind her without protest, but not without one more longing glance at the tea cart just as the door separated him from the repast.

The room fell silent. Virginia had nothing to say to the brat who was about to ruin a once-in-a-lifetime opportunity for her.

"Tea?" She heard him offer.

How dare he speak to me? "Thank you, no." *And I don't care how clipped my voice sounds. Serves him right. He needs to know exactly how I feel about his nose in my business — no matter how handsome he is.* Virginia twisted as far as she could towards the window, pretending to observe something far more interesting than that which stood behind her, offering her sawdust muffins and tepid tea.

Moments passed and thankfully, Rory didn't attempt further communication with her.

Virginia nearly jumped out of her skin when there came a crashing sound from the room in which Beatrice and Luke were discussing what was likely her fate, as if a small table and its bric-à-brac had met in a brutal fashion with the floor. She turned towards the door expecting to see either of them emerge. When no one appeared, Virginia returned her gaze to the window. Luke must have been making hasty love to Beatrice in the next room. Even after as long as they'd been married and through the entire time Virginia had lived with them, it was clear to her that they still desired each other with a violent, tangible passion. *How romantic.* Virginia could only dream she'd find that kind of love someday.

Rory cleared his throat, obviously uncomfortable about the activity's clamour. The commotion from the other room seeped through the walls, but not in the form of words. It was more like a low singing, intermittent and difficult to determine exactly whose voice it was.

Rory started to whistle some indiscriminate tune, then proceeded to take great interest in buttering each muffin on the plate. Each time the inhuman music sounded from the other room, Rory whistled louder.

Virginia had to press her lips together to keep from laughing at his discomfort.

The moment a climactic note sounded from the off-stage duet, Rory coughed into a napkin for what seemed like an overly long time.

Virginia stood to pound him on the back, when all went quiet.

As there wasn't a scrap of food left to butter, Rory hovered near the tea cart, shoulders stiff as if everything breakable in the room was about to shatter.

Virginia returned to the window seat. *Don't tell me he's turned into a prude since that day all those years ago.*

He started like a nervous cat when Luke and Beatrice emerged from the room. Beatrice patted the back of her hair and took a seat next to Virginia, while Luke went for the tea tray. Rory's hands fisted on his hips and he shot Luke an odd, reprimanding glance. Luke shrugged, grinned and bit into a muffin.

Why on earth was Rory acting so strange? She glanced about the room at Luke's lazy smile and Beatrice's flushed cheeks. It was romantic. Terribly so. Virginia would donate two dozen prize-winning sweet cheese pastries to find out if Rory's social interaction had remained limited ever since the infamous, unchaperoned carriage ride. Perhaps living with his elderly aunt all those years had stolen the joy from his life.

"Luke and I have just been discussing what seems to be a source of friction in this family. We" —her gaze briefly touched Luke then Rory—"all of us, are very proud of Virginia and her accomplishments, and hold in the highest regard the grand opportunity she's won in France."

Virginia sat up just a tad straighter.

"However, the majority of us agree that she should take a companion with her."

Before Virginia could react, Beatrice continued, "As such, since both of us have been reassured that the two of you have acknowledged...the decisions of your youth as...no longer *operative*, Luke and I have made the decision to allow Rory to accompany Virginia on the trip as her chaperone."

A strangled sound issued from Rory's throat.

Virginia shot to her feet. "What?" *Oh, no. Please. Not him.* She bit down on her tongue to stop her thoughts from being voiced as Beatrice had instructed during the first few years she'd come to live with her and Luke. *He'll be intrusive…he…he'd never let me be. He'd be underfoot constantly, and I can't have that sort of distraction while I work. Cooking is a delicate matter, and he's a…a bull in a house of china cups.*

"Ace, you can't really mean —"

Luke cut in on Rory just before stuffing the last morsel of muffin between his lips. "We do, actually."

Beatrice stood. "We'll pay you, Rory."

"Pay —?" Virginia choked.

"The same rate per month you received from Aunt Iris." Beatrice nodded.

"Do forgive me, dearest sister-in-law, but this is impossible." Rory shook his head. "I don't need money. Aunt Iris left me her entire estate not five weeks ago."

"Yes, and because your social calendar is now clear for the rest of the summer, you will accompany Virginia to France."

"But I don't want —"

Luke dived into the conversation again. "No, you don't want it, but you'll do it. It was your idea for Virginia to have a companion after all, and who better for the job?"

Virginia cleared her throat and stepped toward the feuding relatives. "I'd appreciate it if you didn't speak of me as if I weren't in the room." After everyone murmured their contrition, she continued. "Is this the only way I'm to gain the blessing of my family — by having *Mr Hughson* the younger, breathing down my apron at every moment of the day?"

For a brief moment, Virginia caught Beatrice's near-grin, but she recovered just in time to reply, "I would have put it more diplomatically but yes, that is exactly the situation."

Now it was Virginia's internal oven that was near the broiling point and she could feel the heat rising from the top of her head. How dare they, those she trusted and loved more than her very own life, enforce this rule upon her? She turned to Rory. Her vision tunnelled, his face seemed to float at the end. She pointed at him, feeling much like the *Ghost of Christmas Yet to Come*, staring down her finger as if it were a sight on a rifle. "If you so much as stir the air around me while I'm working, I'll make goulash out of you!"

Rory's gaze skimmed the ceiling then came to rest on his brother. "Now, how am I supposed to work with *that*?"

Luke's lips twitched. "Hmm. I've never had goulash."

* * * *

Virginia lounged on a deck chair in the sun, a book of recipes in her lap, a large straw bonnet and chiffon scarf protecting her face from the elements. The steam ship bound for France didn't pitch to and fro as badly as she thought it would.

"A fine day for a stroll, wouldn't you say, Miss Clark?"

From beneath the brim of her hat, her gaze travelled the length of a pair of very male, trouser-clad legs, barely slipping past the midsection that sprouted into a luscious V, landing on the man's square, freshly-shaven jaw. Her tummy gave a bit of a flutter. Even with the breath of the Atlantic Ocean ruffling her skirts, she could smell his cedar and crisp-linen soap.

Her life had finally come together and now, the only man who could release her untamed heart from its socially enforced restraints had sauntered back into her life. She squinted at his face.

"Aren't you supposed to be in steerage?"

"I upgraded myself, thank you very much."

Virginia returned her attention to her book. Perhaps he'd get the hint that she wasn't in the mood for conversation of any sort — or to have her carefully laid foundation of societal manners shaken to the core.

The scraping of a chair's legs across the wooden deck made her teeth clench. Rory settled himself into the retrieved chaise longue at her right as if she'd invited him.

A server came by and offered them tall glasses of mint julep, which Virginia declined and Rory accepted.

Rory sat nursing his drink, not uttering a word, for a good quarter of an hour, and the entire time, Virginia contemplated if there could be a large enough pie crust made to encase him, a few hundred cups of mushroom gravy and a dozen or so bushels of root vegetables.

"Having been charged with this duty, I am going to approach it with the utmost solemnity. I shall be there for you at every turn."

Her gaze snapped to his. "You do, Rory Hughson, and I'll draw and quarter you and serve you in place of a fish course!"

His face reddened. "You are choiceless in this matter. You will either accept my assistance or we sail back to New York."

When she couldn't find the words to do battle with him, her fingers strangled the book in her hands.

Virginia refused to further acknowledge his presence. Didn't he know that he wasn't needed here? She wasn't in any moral danger, for Heaven's sake. She shifted in her chair and tried for the tenth time to focus on the recipe before her. Damn if she couldn't think when he was near. This had better not set a precedent for her summer or she'd fail for sure.

Frustrated, she slammed the book shut and stood. Rory set down his empty glass and stood as well, but before she could escape, he placed a hand upon her arm.

She raised her gaze to his.

"Virginia, I…"

"You are going to ruin everything. Why are you here?"

"I…I beg your pardon?"

"Why are you here, Rory?"

His jaw hardened like granite. "You know precisely why I'm here."

"But I don't need you."

He tipped his head slightly and an insolent lock of hair fell to dangle over his forehead. "Don't need me or don't *want* me?"

She stared at him and realised only too late that her mouth had opened and closed a few times, like a carp pulled from a lake. How could the rat make her so nervous? "What is that supposed to mean?"

"What does it sound like?"

Loath to stumble over the slightest pause at this point in their conversation, she turned on her heel. "Go home, Mr Hughson," she shot over her shoulder and turned the corner to take the stairs to her cabin.

Virginia slammed the door and sagged against it, hugging the recipe book to her chest. She didn't need a bloody chaperone... Wait, did he just hint that he wanted her to want him?

"Impossible," she murmured over the sound of her pounding heart. A proper chaperone would never suggest such a thing. Then again, he wasn't, nor had he ever been very proper.

Her cheeks heated to a simmer. "No. Not at all proper."

Chapter Three

Following the brief exchange on deck, Virginia had, for the most part, stayed in her cabin for the remainder of the sea voyage. Early on she'd begrudgingly accepted the fact that Rory wouldn't just go away but that he'd stay for the duration of the summer. Now, as they sat facing each other in the private vis-à-vis carriage sent by Monsieur Gaston Leroux, the host for the summer party, Virginia felt as if her nerves were about to unravel. She'd been so intent upon memorising dessert recipes that she'd forgotten to think of how she would present Rory to Monsieur Leroux without appearing buffoonish.

"You look very pretty," Rory said above the clip-clop of the horses' hooves.

Virginia snapped her gaze to his. *Just what sort of trouble does he think to stir up now, for Heaven's sake?* She needed to focus on her job.

He tugged at one of his sleeve cuffs. "You don't have to scowl at me, you know. I was just trying to ease your anxiety."

"There is no need for you to comfort me. I'm fine. Just fine." She nodded once to confirm her point.

"Truly? Then why are your fingers twisted into knots?"

Virginia released her tingling fingers from the unwitting death grip she'd had on them and smoothed out her skirt. "Besides, I'm not here to look pretty, I'm here to do a job for Monsieur Leroux. Or have you forgotten?"

"You are a woman." He shrugged. "Aunt Iris always said that no matter what any woman does in life, she'll wish to look pretty doing it." His gaze travelled to where her hands rested on her thighs, then languidly made its way back to her face.

She squirmed under such direct scrutiny. "Well, I don't care. I just want to be the best pastry chef France has ever seen."

Luke chuckled. "I vow they will eat whatever you put in front of them."

Amusement bubbled up inside her at his terribly uninformed statement. "Serving them 'whatever' is not my goal." Without doubt, the last time they found themselves in a carriage alone, the situation had been altogether different. Virginia refused to think of that now. Her feelings were sure to show on her face. She recited the table of liquid measurements to herself to divert her thoughts.

He folded his arms over his chest. "I've made an observation."

Congratulations. As her thought remained unspoken, he must have assumed she wanted to hear more.

"Out of everyone who participated in your graduating class, you won. And do you know why?"

"Yes. Because I'm good at what I do."

"No. Because like most of the male population, this benefactor finds you attractive."

"Impossible. What an exaggeratory statement."

"Indeed? Why?"

"Because for your information, Monsieur Leroux and I didn't meet until after I'd won the contest!"

She watched Rory's mouth open, expecting some foolish retort. But he didn't utter a word. She had him this time. Thoroughly satisfied with her statement and its effect upon her superfluous chaperone, she turned towards the lowered window and closed her eyes against the warm breeze. In order to enter the contest it had been required that all contestants submit a photograph of themselves. However, the statement that she and Monsieur Leroux had not met prior to the announcement of the winner had been quite true.

Honestly. It didn't matter who saddled the horse, there was a journey to be taken and she was bloody well going to take it. And she'd be double-baked if she'd let Rory Hughson stand in her way.

Virginia tapped the toe of her foot on the floor of the carriage. What in blazes would she tell Monsieur Leroux about Rory, that he was her brother? No. There wasn't a shred of resemblance to be found. That he was a friend? No. Without doubt they would appear to be lovers to her employer. He had no education in the culinary arts. He certainly couldn't help her with —

She gasped. "That's it! I've got it!"

"Got what?"

"You, Mr Hughson, are my new apprentice."

"I'm — I'm what?"

She drew her bottom lip between her teeth and smiled, utterly pleased with herself.

Rory shifted in his seat. "I don't trust that grin on your face."

Her shoulders relaxed. "Since you insisted on intruding upon my summer position, I am going to make you my assistant. We'll play like you are interested in personal instruction and wish for a culinary career. Yes, that's perfect. The tiny fib will legitimise your conspicuous presence."

"What exactly will you have me doing?"

"Oh—" She was unable to hide her amusement. "This and that."

"I think I'll pass."

"You are choiceless in this matter," she said with nothing short of the smugness she felt. "Just as I had none in your decision to tag along."

"I do have a choice. I won't do it and that's final."

"Have you a better idea? One that won't ruin my reputation or make me look like some little lost child in need of a chaperone?"

Virginia could see the wheels in his head grinding away like a mill. He made to speak a few times, but not a single word passed over his lips.

"There. You see? You will just have to play along—unless you'd like to turn around and get yourself back to America."

He mumbled something incoherent that sounded suspiciously like reluctant conformity.

"Good. I'm glad you agree."

Rory glared at her, his fathomless blue eyes stormy. She smiled to herself and imagined he would remain rather dissatisfied for the remainder of the trip. If not, she'd see to it by reminding him of his new place in this world.

* * * *

"Ah, Mademoiselle Clark. I'm so glad you have arrived safely." Monsieur Leroux stood and came around his desk. He took Virginia's hand and pressed a kiss across her knuckles.

"*Merci*, Monsieur Leroux. May I introduce my assistant, Mr Hughson." Virginia had her well-prepared speech ready to explain Rory's presence. However, Monsieur Leroux barely spared him a glance.

"Fine, fine. Follow the main hallway all the way to the rear of the chateau just past the dining room. Therein, you will find that the kitchen staff rooms are accessible from the stairs to the right of the pantry. I have a few more details to settle for my summer party, so if you will excuse me."

He bowed sending them both on their way with far less pomp than Virginia had expected. She'd been so concerned about Rory's presence, she'd not even got a better look at the man—no better than the first time they had met just after the contest. It had been as brief as the few words they'd exchanged three seconds ago. Not that she minded all that much. He was, after all, her employer and wealthy men tended to be on the peculiar side.

* * * *

Frustrated, Rory punched an already flattened pillow in his small room in the servant's wing at Château Leroux. They'd driven all day and into the evening to reach the grand mansion, and the brief reception he and Ginny had received from the host of the party was less than notable. They were introduced and dismissed nearly in the same breath.

In addition, Rory hadn't slept a wink in the carriage. Having Ginny at close quarters for that amount of time only served to stir his senses to agonising life, leaving him with a wretched, dull ache in his unwittingly-stimulated groin. All he could smell for a day and a half was a hint of orange blossoms mixed with her uniquely feminine scent. How many times today had he wanted to snatch that smart little hat of hers from her head and loose her satiny chestnut tresses to spill over his hands and down her shoulders?

What on earth made him think he could pull this off? He'd lied to his own brother about his not having feelings for Ginny. To tell the honest truth, he was simply lost in her big, sparkling brown eyes, helpless when her wit snapped like the end of a whip and mesmerised by her full, pouting lips. Not that she'd pouted much. In fact, since the carriage ride to the Leroux château, she'd grinned like a cat that'd stolen the cream. Lord, how he'd love for her to lick the cream off his—

A knock sounded at his door, bringing him out of his lusty musings.

"Mr Hughson? Are you decent?"

It was Ginny, and no, he was far from decent. He might as well have been holding a sign that read, 'I'm as hard as a rail spike' with a road sign pointing to the crotch of his tented trousers. "One moment, please."

He paced the room to the window and back again. *Aunt Iris. Aunt Iris's silver tea service. Aunt Iris and her friends. Aunt Iris' friends naked.*

He took a deep, cleansing breath and spewed it across the room. "I'm decent now." Presentably deflated he tugged open the door.

Ginny held out a covered tray to him which he promptly took up. "Report to me in the kitchen tomorrow morning at five-thirty. We will meet the head chef and begin breakfast preparations then."

"Do me a favour?"

She spun on her heel to walk away, but stopped when he spoke. She turned her head but didn't face him. "And what is that?"

"Call me Rory. I think we've been through enough together to earn the privilege."

She expelled an annoyed huff. "Fine. Rory. Do not be late." And with that she stalked away.

Rory toed the door closed and set his supper down on a small table.

So. Miss Ginny Clark thought herself in charge. Didn't she realise she was a mere female attempting to penetrate the unshakable male-dominated culinary system, in conformist France, no less? She needed his help more than she knew, although if he displeased her, he'd bet she could distribute the discipline quicker than one could blink. And he might let her, too, he grinned.

* * * *

The head chef had spoken to the kitchen entirely in French. Luckily, Ginny had taken two years of the language at Wellesley. There had been only a few words here and there she hadn't recognised. She didn't let on to Chef Auguste that she'd understood most of his address, especially after he'd given her the once-over towards the end of his illustrious speech with that steely-eyed gaze of his.

The self-imposed snobbishly French superiority of the head chef supplied only half of the problem. Rory

29

hadn't bothered to show up. Originally, she'd wanted him to stay away from the kitchen, to stay hidden from everyone she'd need to work with. But once the brilliant idea had taken hold in her mind and she'd gone ahead and mentioned her so-called assistant to Monsieur Leroux the night before, she expected Rory to at least pretend to play the part.

She shook the anger off and headed for the pantry, intent on seeing what ingredients she had to work with until she could compile her own menus, attach a list for market and turn it in to Chef Auguste.

The kitchen itself was a marvel. Three immense, half-circle lead-crystal windows graced the south wall, allowing ample sunlight in during the day. The burnt-orange tiled floor dotted with tiny cream squares appeared free of any dust or debris, and the white stucco walls supported a high ceiling with thick wooden beams crisscrossing the length of the room. It boasted no fewer than four ovens of various sizes, which sat beneath the windows, two deep sinks equipped with hot and cold running water, numerous shelves and bakers' racks and pots and pans in copper and cast iron of every dimension imaginable. Down the centre of the room sat an enormous wooden chopping block that served as the main food preparation area, and above hung all sorts of culinary tools. It was a chef's dream kitchen.

The pantry was big enough to house a king's wardrobe. However, Virginia felt it was terribly unorganised. In the midst of assessing the amount of flour stored in a large oaken barrel kept upon a very high shelf, she heard someone whistling.

Virginia almost toppled from the stepladder. It was Rory, and he was whistling *Dixie*.

She stopped him as he passed the door to the pantry. "Are you insane?" she hissed.

"Well. Good morning to you, too." He grinned and leaned against the doorframe.

"Don't patronise me! First of all, you are late. You missed the head chef's welcome speech and lastly, don't whistle in the kitchen. You sound like a crass American!"

"I am a—"

Virginia shook a pointed finger in his direction. "Don't you dare say it! If you muddle this opportunity for me I swear I'll—"

Their heated debate was brought to an abrupt halt when a series of rapid-fire tuts clicked from behind Rory. "Americans," Chef Auguste murmured in English, then continued. His voice sounded calm but he scolded them as if they were children. "I will not tolerate arguments in my kitchen." He then turned to Virginia. "What will you prepare for Monsieur Leroux to fortify him for the arrival of his guests this afternoon?"

She adopted a serene smile. "I thought I'd make crêpes, Chef."

An irritatingly smug grin flattened his lips. "How...unique." Then he turned on his heel and left the room.

Virginia closed her eyes and hoped the breath would return to her lungs before she fell over from lack of oxygen to the brain. *So, Chef found my idea 'unique', eh?* She could play his game, he just didn't know it yet.

"He's not very friendly, is he?"

She chuckled at Rory's observation. "His job isn't to be friendly, he's the head chef. Perhaps he thinks he must appear the ogre in order to gain respect."

"Were I the head chef, I'd—"

"Well, you're not. You're not even the garbage boy at this point."

Rory shrugged, which irritated her further. She huffed out a breath. "Look, just—go down to cold storage and bring me about a half-cup of *fromage frais*."

"What, where…?"

She raised her gaze in supplication to the kitchen gods. "Go out the back door and follow the path to the right until you get to the set of wooden storm doors which slant into the ground. Enter and go down the stairs. The wine cellar will be on the left, the cold storage on the right. You'd already know the way had you been more punctual this morning."

He obviously ignored her reprimand. "And I'm to fetch what?"

"*Fromage frais*. It's white, unaged cheese. I've decided to prepare Hungarian *palacsintas* instead of crêpes. He wants unique? I'll serve it to him fried."

Chapter Four

Gaston Leroux closed his eyes as if in ecstasy and chewed the bite of Ginny's Hungarian dish—which looked suspiciously like crêpes to Rory. He dabbed the corner of his lips with a linen napkin. "You are truly *mon chou ange.*"

Ginny blushed prettily, damn it all. She'd not done that for Rory since —

"*Merci,* Monsieur Leroux." She beamed. "*Bon appetit.*"

Rory followed Ginny out of the dining room. "Why are you making his breakfast? I thought you were a pastry chef?" He hadn't meant to grumble, but the Frenchman irritated him to no end.

"The task falls to me because of the small staff Monsieur Leroux and Chef have assembled. I not only provide desserts and breads, but also breakfast. In addition, I've been selected to assist with the pantry."

"Selected? You sound happy that they've added more to your list of duties."

She spun around, stopping him in his tracks. "Had Chef not found me capable, he would have given the job to someone else."

"I think he means to belittle you. Any half-wit servant can make a list of supplies and go to market."

"I didn't say I would go to mark—" She threw her hands in the air. "Oh, never mind."

Her eyes flashed at him and she stormed off. She was so adorable when she was miffed.

They arrived at the kitchen and found that someone had cleaned up. "Excellent, the dish faery must be smiling down on us."

"Don't worry. We'll be paying her back, I promise you that."

"But now we are free for the afternoon."

Ginny chuckled and entered the pantry. "Free? Sir, I hate to disappoint you, but we need to make the bread for tonight's meal, not to mention dessert."

"But supper is hours away," he scoffed, watching her from the doorway.

"Just how long do you think it takes to make bread?" she asked and ascended the step ladder, placing a hand upon the large flour barrel.

He paused, doing the math in his head. "An hour?"

Her laughter sparkled over him from high atop her perch. "It will take at least that for the dough to rise." She grabbed the top of the barrel and in the blink of an eye, lost her balance. Rory leapt forward, catching Ginny with one arm and, miraculously, the barrel with the other.

He held her tight. "Are you all right?" he asked and eased the still-sealed barrel down the length of his leg to the floor. Unable to resist, he snaked his other hand around her waist and he pulled her closer. He buried his nose in her hair and inhaled.

"I am." She seemed out of breath, like that day on the way to Tucson. The blood surged in his veins. She felt so right against him. Damn good thing he was there to catch her, too.

The woman in his arms made a sound somewhere between a whimper and a cough. He splayed his hands across her back but when she spoke, he realised his mistake.

"Release me."

It was a simple statement, delivered devoid of malice or demand. Without question, he carried out her bidding.

He watched Ginny study the floor intently. "I...I thank you for your service, but must ask that if you are called upon to do such again, please do so without the intimacy you displayed just now." Her voice could have passed for a light breeze.

Rory was hard pressed to detect any emotion in her request whatsoever, a testament to how much she must loathe him. Damnation, she wouldn't even look at him. He buried tight fists deep into the pockets of his trousers and nodded. "Fine. My apologies."

Virginia couldn't escape the kitchen fast enough. She needed to saturate her lungs with air that didn't fill her senses with fresh-from-the-oven bread mixed with the scent of Rory Hughson. Her room was her only refuge. He wouldn't dare follow her in there.

She'd endured baking four substantial loaves of crusty sourdough bread under his intimate regard, and in addition, instructed him to prepare the whipped cream for this evening's dessert. The crew assigned to lunches had come and gone — she'd barely tasted the soup they'd served. The kitchen seemed steeped in chaotic activity the entire time. Chef's watchful, critical eye stirred up the staff's nerves. And now the dinner hour rapidly closed down upon them.

Rory had been more than just an assistant. He'd been the perfect gentleman. To her, his mere presence in the kitchen nearly over-shadowed that of Chef. Rory had saved her from injury and embarrassment in the pantry, and had done it in such a gallant, romantic manner she'd nearly swooned.

Virginia groaned and shook her head. Her current thought process would never do. Her head should be clear as she prepared her dishes. She need not think about how close her handsome apprentice stood, how his hand brushed hers when he passed her the requested ingredients or how his eyes seemed to see through to her very soul. Could she bear the next few months at such close proximity to him?

Almost every time she looked at him, he reminded her of that damn carriage ride and each time her resolve wavered, her inhibitions begged to be set free. She couldn't allow herself to slip back into the recklessness of her youth. The consequences would be devastating to her. Everything she had worked for, all her efforts of reining in her girlish fantasies about Rory Hughson would dissolve into dust.

I cannot let him get to me. I'll just have to dive into this job head-first.

Resolve guiding her every step, Virginia strode over to her small writing desk. Chef had requested her menus before the dinner bell rang and she was determined to get them to him free of flaws and on time, if not early. In the midst of teaching Rory how to whip the cream, she'd heard that Monsieur Leroux's guests had all arrived. Each in turn, Chef sent up refreshment trays, and they had come back without a single significantly-sized crumb. Obviously, Chef knew what he was doing.

Virginia gathered her pantry list and menus and tucked them neatly into a smart leather wallet she'd purchased in New York. Before she reached for the door, she took a relaxing breath, readying herself for more of Rory's close-quartered company.

Upon entering the kitchen, she saw Chef and Madame Simone, the *Potager*, who also doubled as the *Saucier*, hovering over a large cauldron at the main stoves. Madame Simone's grey hair was tucked snugly beneath her toque, as Chef had requested of her none too gently earlier in the day. The older woman had complied without hesitation, her hazel gaze not once flashing the ire she likely felt over Chef's indelicacy.

On the opposite side of the kitchen near the great hearth, she found Rory sitting on a stool with a pretty little serving girl buzzing around him like a bee. Virginia stepped closer to hear what they were saying.

"Is your arm in much pain?" the blonde sympathised with a French accent like heavy, sweet cream.

"The muscles of my arm are cramping something awful."

Oh, brother. Virginia's gaze scraped the ceiling. He hadn't whined, but the tone of his voice begged for attention.

"Are you not used to whipping things so thoroughly, then?" The girl's double entendre didn't evade Virginia's notice, one would have had to be a simpleton not to spot it. "I could help you with practice, perhaps show you a better method?" She slid her fingers down his offended forearm.

Rory grinned at her.

"Ahem." Virginia was not ashamed of her phony clearing of the throat. It had gained Rory's attention quite effectively.

He stood. Guilt flashed in his eyes, then melted like butter. "I didn't see you come in," he murmured.

"Obviously," Virginia responded flatly. She then turned to the serving girl. "I can attest to the fact that he's been whipping things on his own for years." She thought she'd heard Rory choke, but ignored the strangled sound.

The girl gave Rory one last glance before she stuck her nose in the air at Virginia and flounced off.

"I'm finally shown some kindness and you go and shoo her away." Rory pouted.

"Leave it to you to give kindness marks to a tart."

"You didn't have to be so...so..."

"What, truthful?"

"No, so harsh."

"Oh, please. Had I not been ensconced in the hierarchy of the kitchen, I'm sure she would have offered to scratch my eyes out." Not allowing Rory to comment, she continued. "Now, tell me, does your arm really hurt?"

Rory shrugged.

"Good. Now, let us finish the dessert. You fetch the cream you whipped from the cold storage, and..."

"Um, it's gone."

"Gone? What do you mean, 'gone'?"

"It seems Chef needed it for the soup. I watched him enter with Madame Simone and he had the bowl. Before I could say anything, he'd scooped the cream into that huge black pot."

Virginia could feel the heat rising from the top of her head. She turned and strode toward the main stoves,

praying she wouldn't burst like too much fruit filling
sealed into a non-ventilated pie crust.

C h a p t e r   F i v e

"Chef, may I see you for a moment?" She felt proud that her voice didn't reveal the seething anger churning in her belly. With an air of nonchalance she awaited his reply.

"*Dans un moment, s'il vous plait,*" he said without even looking at her.

Virginia gritted her teeth. She could have poached a dozen individual eggs before he turned to face her.

"Now, what is it you want?"

She forced a smile. "First I'd like to present you with my menus." She handed him the wallet.

Chef made a face as if he smelt something foul. He opened the wallet, removed the papers then tossed the wallet into the nearest garbage container. "I will look at these later," he murmured and jammed them into the front pocket of his apron.

Shocked at his actions, Virginia somehow kept her composure. "I'd also like to ask you…" No. She would not sound offended. He'd slap her on the wrist for sure if she did. "What I mean is, I'm glad you found the whipped cream useful." She caught Madame Simone's glance and could sense her silent apology.

Chef harrumphed. "*Oui*. Seeing that it was not yet sweetened, I knew you wouldn't need it." He turned back to Madame Simone and the soup, dismissing Virginia like a serf.

She fisted her hands into balls at her sides. She'd not added the sugar because she had been too focused on teaching Rory the whipping technique she'd learned at school. Well, she would not make that mistake again. She stalked back to Rory, bid him take up another whisk and bowl, and follow her to the cold storage.

"That man is unbelievable!" she bellowed after Rory shut the cold storage door with them inside. He could just make out her figure by the light of the candle she'd set upon a shelf. "He's arrogant, self-absorbed and thinks he can do no wrong!"

"He's French." Rory had stated the obvious and yet it made her laugh. The sound rolled over him like a warm summer breeze.

"I've met French people before, but never one like him," she commented while replacing a sliver of ice with a new block atop the butter crock.

"This is your first time in France, no?" Rory said with a phony French accent, which made Ginny giggle again.

"You don't seem affected by him," she said and moved towards the cream barrel. "Bring your bowl here."

Rory didn't answer, but did as she bid. Ginny's hand covered his to steady the bowl. He hoped his hand didn't shake from the mere contact with hers. The cool, flesh of her palm gave rise to his longing for her.

He'd managed to keep his adoration at bay, but now his sense of touch had heightened in the near-darkness. How he yearned to toss aside the tools of a cook and press his body to hers as he'd done in the pantry. Since she'd voiced her opinion about his familiarity, she'd been all business, but it hadn't remotely quenched his desire for her.

Ginny ladled two helpings of cream into the bowl. "Now, whip it into a cloud just as you did earlier," she instructed and took up her candle once again.

As he whipped the cream hard and fast, they walked back up and entered the kitchen's pantry where Virginia sprinkled sugar into the bowl at intervals.

"Very well, you can stop. It looks stiff enough."

Oh, she has no idea.

She dipped a finger into the fluffy white mass and popped it into her mouth. He watched with fascination how her lips wrapped around that slim digit of hers. His blood roared to life and headed like a freight train straight for his groin.

Her head tilted the slightest bit to the side and she tested it again with another finger. Rory was sure he'd stopped breathing.

"Yes." She nodded. "That will do." She took the bowl from him and gave him permission to sample what remained on the whisk.

He brought the wire whisk to his mouth and stuck out his tongue for a lick. Their creation was sweet and cool. "This would go great on..." Thank God he'd stopped before finishing with 'your skin'.

"Great on...?"

He swallowed. "Just about anything."

"Yes, well, tonight it's going on strawberries. Come, we must see to said berries before Chef dumps them into the soup. And Rory?"

"Yes?"

"Thank you for making light of...what we discussed earlier. It helps me retain my sanity just to have someone to rail at when I need to, someone who I can depend upon to keep my feelings to himself."

Rory nodded. He'd be beholden to the gods if he could find a way to be indispensable to her for the entire summer. Perhaps then she'd be less inclined to dismiss him once they arrived home.

* * * *

Dinner had been a success in the eyes of Monsieur Leroux and his guests, but in Chef's exalted and none too discreet opinion, Virginia was a less-than-adequate *pâtissier*.

"Strawberries and whipped crème. The American seems to have outdone herself," he'd commented flatly right to her face. "And by the way, I will be returning half of your recipes as they are hopeless."

Chef's words rang in her head like the aftertaste of pungent cheese lingered on the tongue. *What an arrogant ass.* She harrumphed. If he had his druthers, he'd probably demote her to server. In fact, she was sure now that Chef had given her the pantry position only to give her more to do, just like Rory had suggested. Well, she wouldn't break down. She was much stronger than the arrogant Frenchman assumed.

What lay before Virginia would take up every spare moment for at least two weeks. Eventually, she'd have to see what she could come up with to replace the recipes that had dissatisfied Chef, however, right now breakfast preparations beckoned.

Was she supposed to guess which recipes Chef had rejected? Virginia wiped her forehead on a rag and tossed it into a basket. She turned to the pantry with a huff.

Just then, she felt a hand at her elbow. "The pots and pans are finally finished. Why don't we go for a walk?"

Oh, how she'd love to steal away in the moonlight with Rory. If anyone could ease her tension it was he, but alas. She faced him. "I'm sorry, I can't. I have to prepare for tomorrow."

He released her arm. "When do you sleep?" he asked, irritation tainting his tone.

"In between the first and second courses."

"I'm serious, Ginny."

Had there not been a few kitchen workers hovering over left-over crusts of bread, she probably would have given in to him, especially after he'd used her childhood nickname, which she should've admonished him for. On the way to Tucson, he'd whispered it repeatedly while kissing her. She brought herself out of the memory. "You mustn't call me that," she murmured. Turning on her heel, she entered the pantry.

Chapter Six

It must have been midnight by the time they'd finished cutting up berries and combining ingredients for the morning's Scandinavian waffles. They were alone in the kitchen and Rory noticed how Ginny's head dipped every so often, indicating how tired she was. On their last trip to cold storage she'd stumbled on the pathway twice.

"You haven't been sleeping well, have you?"

Ginny responded with a shrug. She placed a stack of crystal breakfast plates behind a large black cauldron then reached for the heart-shaped waffle iron.

"Look, you can barely lift that iron. Why don't you go on to bed and I'll set things out for tomorrow?"

"Thank you for the offer, but I need to make sure everything is accounted for." Carefully, Ginny placed the iron on a low shelf and covered it with an old table cloth.

He chuckled. "You say that as if things will sprout legs and walk away in the middle of the night."

"Like the whipped cream did this afternoon?" she asked and stood back to survey her efforts.

She had a point. "Do you suspect deliberate sabotage?"

She sighed, untied her apron and used it as a hand towel. "As much as I hate to admit it, I do not trust Chef." She shook her head. "At school, along with cooking, we practised peace and harmony in the kitchen, not condescension and scheming pretext. For instance, I would have never used someone else's ingredients without first confirming they weren't to be used."

"I see your point."

They put out the last of the lamps and started up the servant's stairs. Faint moonlight shone through long, clear glass windows, guiding their steps. "I can't let him intimidate me to the point of ruination," she said when they reached her door. "I must overcome this. I must succeed."

Ginny was near to tears, her lack of sleep likely not helping matters. Rory wanted to take her in his arms and hold her, but he knew she'd only become angry. He made to sweep a hand down her arm but stopped himself just in time. "If there is anything I can do to help, let me know. I promise to keep vigil as much as possible."

"Thank you," she whispered and slipped into her room, shutting the door behind her.

Rory strode over to his door and entered his small room. *Poor girl. She's taken too much upon herself.*

* * * *

"Here's to three entire weeks of brilliant breakfasts and desserts." Rory lifted his half-full glass of champagne and clinked it to Virginia's equally proportioned one.

"Thank you." She sipped and swallowed. "And shame on you for stealing this celebratory beverage."

Rory chuckled. "I didn't steal it, it was about to be discarded. I dare say I saved it from a terrible fate. This is damn fine champagne."

"It is. And expensive, too. Monsieur Leroux insists on serving only perfectly chilled *Veuve Clicquot*. He raves about how —"

The doors that led to the corridor, which separated the kitchen from the rest of Château Leroux, burst open. Rory snatched the glass from her hand, tucking both drinks behind his back. Chef, with two servers in tow, marched up to Virginia and practically tossed her creation upon the counter in front of her. "Is the American so stupid that she doesn't know to serve brandied raspberries over custard *a la flambé*?"

She reached out and took hold of the counter so not to topple over. Heat flared in her cheeks and she drew in a deep breath to chase away the tunnel vision. "*A la flambé* is — is merely a choice — it's not at all required."

"*Absurde*. Get another dessert in there in three minutes or you are finished. I must go now and apologise for your idiocy." With that he stormed back through the doors, the two servers followed in his wake.

Virginia's gaze wandered over the unmolested dishes. She wondered if Chef had even allowed them to be set upon the table. "The bastard," she hissed.

"What can I do to help?" Rory asked, setting the champagne glasses down.

"How dare he? What right has he got?" She spun and stalked into the pantry. Snatching a bottle of cognac from the shelf she brought it out to her dishes.

"Fetch me a wick," she tossed at Rory, while opening the bottle.

By the time he returned with a lit wick, each custard dish was sufficiently saturated with cognac.

"Shall I—" he began.

"No. Let me. Wheel the cart over." They set the desserts on the cart. She took the wick from him and in seconds the dishes were engulfed in flame.

Virginia rushed them into the dining room, aware and terribly happy that Rory had followed her.

Without even a glance at Chef Auguste, whom she saw retreating into a far corner upon her entrance, Virginia set the dishes in front of Monsieur Leroux's guests.

The recipients of the desserts broke into applause.

The built-up anxiety was almost too much to bear. She laughed and presented a pretty curtsy. She and Rory put out the dishes with dome lids amidst murmured praise. She turned to go when Monsieur Leroux stopped her.

"Mademoiselle Clark, I must commend you on your delicious works. I'm so glad you decided to serve us yourself this time."

If Monsieur Leroux would have asked her to marry him, she would have said yes. "*Merci*, Monsieur." She grinned. "You don't know how much that means to me."

"*Amis*, it is about time I introduce you to *mon chou ange*, Mademoiselle Clark. Mademoiselle, this is Monsieur Hector Guimard, an up-and-coming architect here in France."

He stood and she inclined her head to the pleasant-looking young man in his mid-twenties.

"And Antonio de la Gándara, one of the most talented young painters in Barbizon."

Monsieur Gándara came out of his chair. He sported a bushy brown moustache and above his eyes sat similarly bushy eyebrows. "Monsieur," she murmured and nodded to the painter.

"And lastly, Tristan Bernard, our resident novelist."

Monsieur Bernard rose and reached for Virginia's hand. When his fingers enfolded hers, he drew her towards him, taking in every inch of her with his gaze as if making mental notes. "Finally we get to meet Gaston's Pastry Angel." He kissed the back of her hand, his lips lingering longer than necessary.

"Please," she said and reclaimed her limb. "Monsieur Leroux flatters."

"On the contrary, Mademoiselle." Monsieur Leroux chuckled. "The fact is, I'd be willing to risk money that you are the best."

Even as she shook her head in protest, Hector lifted his dessert wine in salute. "You may have your chance, provided you are serious."

Monsieur Leroux eyed his friend. "What are you saying, Hector? I am serious, you know."

"The *Pâtissier de Barbizon* competition is coming up. You could sponsor Mademoiselle Clark."

Antonio drew his hand across his chin and jaw. "Hector, I think we could make some real money here." He nudged the grinning architect with his elbow.

"Please, Monsieurs, don't trouble yourselves over me. I am quite new to all this."

"But you have such a flair with sweets." Monsieur Leroux insisted. "Tell you what, if the opportunity presents itself, I will decide then. In the meantime..." He took up his dessert wine. "A toast to *mon chou ange*, the angel of pastry."

Monsieur Leroux's guests drank to Virginia, and in that moment, her very existence seemed validated. She couldn't help but smile, heat suffusing her cheeks.

"You have my most humble thanks. Now I must take my leave. Please, enjoy your dessert, gentlemen." She bobbed a curtsy and she and Rory departed. Not four steps behind them and seething as they went along the hallway was Chef Auguste, but she refused to acknowledge it.

* * * *

"I want her."

"No."

"Gaston, be reasonable."

"Tristan, I didn't invite her here for your pleasure. I am not some pimp, you know."

"Come now, what's the harm?"

"She *is* quite lovely."

"Stay out of this, Antonio," Gaston warned. "I don't need you encouraging Tristan."

"Had any of you noticed how her apprentice was eyeing us? I felt if I made one move towards her he would have ripped my head off."

"You must be dreaming, Hector. I didn't notice it at all."

"Knowing you, Tristan, you didn't notice anything but her because all the blood was leaving your brain and rushing towards your cock."

"I noticed him. I gave him as much notice as she did."

"Well, from where I was sitting, she kept him in her line of sight the entire time she spoke to us."

"Hector, stick to architecture, it's what you're good at. Relationships are above your notice."

"You don't want a relationship with her, you just want to fuck her."

"Now see here—"

"All right. Enough. I don't want anyone on my staff feeling as if they are working in a brothel. If you want, I'll take you into town and we can visit a cabaret. You will find all the lustful amusements you can handle there."

"I hate having to pay for sex."

Gaston laughed. "Poor Tristan. Perhaps if you weren't so ugly—"

Hector and Antonio chuckled.

* * * *

Back in the kitchen, Virginia felt that she could breathe again.

Rory parked the cart and at the other end of the room and stalked across the terracotta-tiled floor toward her. "You, Miss Clark, are a marvel."

Virginia was so elated, she didn't care if within a matter of seconds Rory would have his arms around her. He wasn't a foot away when the doors to the kitchen came crashing open. She whipped around to find Chef Auguste red-faced with rage.

"You think you are so smart, eh? You think that just because an uneducated oaf says you are great that you are? You are nothing!"

The man was about to explode if she didn't think of something to calm him down. "Chef, I'm sure Monsieur Leroux didn't say those things to belittle or demean your work. He was merely being kind to me."

"But you believed him!"

Is he purposefully goading me? "Now, Chef, be reasonable. I—"

"I knew it! That, Mademoiselle, is where your error lies. A trained monkey can mimic, mime and follow a recipe, what makes you any different than the hairy little animal?"

For weeks she had endured his criticism and barbs, his tittering behind her back, his general lack of respect, but she had to draw the line somewhere. "That will do," Virginia barked, her temper flaring to a broil. "I may be a monkey in your eyes, but I've been trained by the very best chefs in America!" He took a breath to speak but she continued. "And I know my way around the kitchen enough to recognise that you, Monsieur, are nothing but a phony."

"I beg...how dare..." he sputtered.

"That's right. I thought I recognised your methods, but kept my suspicions to myself. Why, you can't even do anything without blatantly emulating the great Antoine Carême's style! So if anyone is a fraudulent, trained monkey around here, Chef Auguste, it's you!"

Chef's face turned a lovely shade of eggplant. "I will not be treated in this manner!" He spun on his heel and stormed back towards the dining room.

Virginia's balled hands shook at her sides, her lungs too collapsed to draw air. "Now I've done it," she whispered. "We may as well go pack our bags, Rory."

"Give me a moment—I know how important this is to you. I might be able to think of something to soothe that beast, make him forgive—maybe even forget."

She turned to face him. "That will mean crawling back to him on my hands and knees—grovelling to him, enduring his barbs again and again for the rest of the summer. No. I can't do it."

"Be patient. Perhaps there can be a compromise." Rory took her by the hand and led through the doors to where Monsieur Leroux and his guests were finishing dessert.

Chapter Seven

"…And so I quit!" Chef blew past Rory and Virginia as they entered the dining room.

Silence greeted their wide eyes and Virginia felt as if she'd been punched in the stomach. She stepped forward, ready to face her dismissal head-on.

Monsieur Leroux's guests stood and quietly filed out of the room through the main doors. Their plates were clean, thank goodness.

She dragged her gaze back to her employer. *Here it comes. My humiliation.*

"Mademoiselle, do not look so stricken," Monsieur Leroux crooned from his seat.

"I'm so sorry, Monsieur." She folded her hands contritely. "I never meant to ruin your party."

To her total puzzlement, Monsieur Leroux shrugged a shoulder as if losing Chef Auguste was of no consequence. "You have not ruined anything. In fact, I believe you have improved upon what is more like an intellectual gathering than a soirée."

Impossible. "H—how?"

"Mademoiselle Clark," he announced, "you are Château Leroux's new head chef."

At first, Virginia was unable to speak. Or breathe, for that matter.

"Does that not please you?" he asked.

"I... I—" She cleared her throat. "I believe I'm quite unqualified, Monsieur."

"Nonsense."

"Truly. For one thing, my dishes could never be anywhere near as fancy as Chef Auguste's."

"Mademoiselle, this matters not to me. If I wanted to eat art, I would take a fork and knife to my gallery."

When she heard Rory behind her, covering his laughter with a cough, she couldn't help but grin, if only for a brief moment.

"Not to worry, for I have much confidence in you." He waved a hand in the air as if to dismiss the subject.

"But I'm not familiar enough with your French food to—"

"Mademoiselle, I am too familiar with French food," he jested. "American food is exotic to me. I would be pleased to have some of your native dishes served to me and my guests."

She stopped herself from gawking at the man. "Perhaps...that is, I suppose I could stir up a few ideas." Then she shook her head. "But certainly not enough to fill the entire summer. I don't think—"

"You have talent, Mademoiselle. Auguste seemed more suited to the military." He smiled. "And unlike Auguste, I am unconcerned about you repeating a dish. If you had the same menu each week, I assure you, you would not hear me complain."

Her cheeks heated at the embarrassing idea. Repeating dishes at that rate would get her tossed out of the culinary arts, not to mention France, *tout de suite*. "I would never do that to you and your guests, Monsieur."

"You can cook anything you wish, as long as you keep the pastries coming—they are a particular weakness for me, *mon chou ange*."

* * * *

Virginia had to gather her thoughts, which seemed to be exploding in a dozen different directions. On the way up the stairs to her room, she saw Chef and most of the kitchen staff marching towards the back door, valises and carpet bags in hand, looking as if they'd hastily packed.

Half-way down the hall, it hit her. She was now Head Chef.

The floor tilted. Two strong hands caught her around the waist.

"Easy, there." Rory's smooth voice buzzed in her ear. He helped her to a bench next to a window.

She drew in the breath she had lost and whispered, "What have I done?"

When he didn't respond, she looked up at him for his answer.

"Um… Re-established the revolution?"

Had the situation not called for the utmost gravity she would have laughed at his quip. "Not. Funny."

"I thought so," he murmured and grinned.

She ignored the Hughson dimple that graced the left side of his mouth. "Rory, what in God's name am I going to do?"

"I seriously doubt you have anything to worry about."

Virginia rose from her seat and gestured to the window with a flailing hand. "He's taken more than half the staff away with him!"

"So hire a new staff."

"You are completely ignorant of how delicately a harmonised kitchen staff must be drawn. It would take weeks of interviews and even more time to evaluate letters of recommendation and assess the potential candidate's credentials." She hadn't meant for the volume of her voice to rise but, much to her embarrassment, it echoed down the hall and likely into the kitchen itself.

"Come, let's discuss this in a more private setting." Rory opened the door to his room and, with an upturned hand, directed her inside.

She strode to the far side of the small room and waited for him to shut the door.

"Now that the remaining staff is unable to hear you—"

"I know, I know. That was terribly unprofessional of me," she muttered contritely. "But what am I going to do? This is dreadful!" She turned to the window, placed her forehead upon the glass pane and sighed.

"I'll tell you what I'd like to do." Sarcasm rang in his quiet voice behind her. "I'd like to get Monsieur Leroux to stop calling you little pet names."

Virginia's back stiffened and her head came up, her hands fisted into tight balls at her sides. She whirled on Rory. "I am about to be blacklisted as a chef and all you care about is that?" The walls of the room seemed to close in on her and she felt the air heating around her as if she were in an oven.

"Look, Ginny, I—"

"Consider yourself dismissed!" she choked out. Virginia practically tore the door from its hinges then slammed it shut behind her.

Back in her own room, she was sure to scuff a pale path on the cherry-stained wood floor.

He has no right whatsoever to be jealous – jealous of my employer no less! She seethed. *It's not as if Rory has made any overtures on my behalf – for Heaven's sake, he's nothing more than a bloody chaperone to me! A chaperone I never wanted in the first place. Oh, if only he'd stayed home.*

Virginia froze. "If he'd stayed home, I'd be here all alone." She drew her bottom lip between her teeth. Good God, aside from Monsieur Leroux, Rory Hughson was her only ally, and she'd just dismissed him! She ran to the door and threw it open. Rory stood before her, his hand raised to knock.

"I... I..." Rory stuttered.

"No, don't. I have to apologise. I was dreadfully mistaken a few moments ago." Virginia tossed her head flippantly. "I'm never quite myself when I get frazzled." She felt heat creep up her neck, embarrassed that she'd tried to make light of the matter. Ignoring her ignited skin, she drew in a shuddering breath. "Please. I... I need you."

Elation. That was the emotion Rory felt at Ginny's declaration, but he couldn't let her know. Not yet. He nodded – a sober action in direct opposition of his soaring heart. "What can I do to help?"

Ginny's furrowed brow relaxed and her pleading look melted into a grateful smile that could have knocked him sideways. The silent chuckles shaking her shoulders weren't too near hysterical, but he could sense the edge was within leaping distance. "There's just so much, I hardly know where to start." She placed her hand on the door frame and slumped to rest her cheek on it.

Rory leaned a shoulder against the other side of the frame. "How about if we start at the beginning?" He reached out and gave her hand a squeeze. Sorely tempted to grin, he stuffed the idea inside like seasoned bread down the neck of a goose.

"Right. The pantry, then."

He let her hand slip from his and she marched passed him. Ginny. His brave little soldier.

When they arrived at the pantry, Madame Simone, Chef Auguste's *Saucier*, stood in the center, paper and pencil in hand.

"Madame Simone, I—"

"*Bonsoir*, Mademoiselle. I thought you might need some assistance with the lists."

"Oh, Madame." She stepped forward as if she was about to throw her arms about the woman, but stopped herself. If Rory hadn't seen her transform into an authority figure before his very eyes, he wouldn't have believed it. Virginia cleared her throat. "Yes, Madame Simone. Thank you. What do we have so far?"

As the two women chatted, Rory felt his heart swell with pride for Ginny. She'd braved the great unknown and now she was going to conquer it. His admiration for her towered over him like thunder clouds, like the French Alps, like...

"And my assistant will accompany me to the markets tomorrow."

Rory snapped out of his reverie at Ginny's words. "Who, me?"

"Of course," she stated with finality and returned her attention to Madame Simone.

He stifled a harrumph. Rory never thought it would be himself to join her in conquering the great unknown, or rather, the grocery markets. Why, he hadn't gone to market since before Aunt Iris passed. He wasn't thrilled with it then and he certainly wasn't happy with the prospect now.

Rory drew in a deep breath to let loose a great sigh. At the top of his breath, Ginny slid him a look that communicated, 'don't even think about it'. He let the inaudible breath flow out through his nose. The girl really could crack the whip. Rory nearly grinned at the thought.

"Mr Hughson."

Rory's gaze met Ginny's. "Yes?"

"I want to you empty this entire pantry. This will make it easier for Madame Simone to inventory the contents. After which, Madame Simone will cleanse the shelving and floor. For now, I want you to place all of the items on the centre table and tomorrow, prior to our trip to market, we'll set it to rights." Before he could protest, Ginny continued. "Meet me here at five a.m. and mind, tardiness will not be tolerated." She pivoted and headed for the stairs.

Rory looked at Madame Simone with a wink. "And you thought Chef Auguste was daunting."

"I heard that!" Ginny yelled from somewhere above stairs.

* * * *

"I think she loves him."

"Nonsense."

"I'm serious, Tristan. Have you seen the way she looks at him? Like the sun doesn't rise without his permission."

"Antonio, you don't know what you are talking about. He's merely her apprentice."

"I know more than you think. You are providing premature answers to the wrong questions. Your approach is unsuitable as well."

"Jealousy isn't very becoming on you, Tristan."

Tristan waved a hand in dismissal of Hector's unflattering comment. "How could I be jealous? I'm not in love with her."

"Such a fine line between lust and love." Antoino chuckled.

"Again, there are words coming out of your mouth but you know not of what you speak. One cannot obtain love without lust setting the spark, but lust can easily exist without love."

Gaston listened to his guests' banter as he swirled brandy in his snifter.

"If you know so very much, Antonio, then tell us. How does he feel about her?"

"That's easy. He loves her as well."

"And you're sure what he feels for her is not merely lust?"

"They seem to know each other well. I would imagine that if you know a woman and can remain good friends, or at the very least, close enough to work alongside her, that such would qualify her to become a cherished companion. That is love."

"What if he's just waiting for the right moment to pounce?"

Hector scoffed. "I'm quite sure he's had ample opportunities to do so."

"Perhaps he's slow in the head."

Gaston cut in. "Our little genius would likely not employ an assistant with mental restrictions. All day they are around sharp objects and hot ovens. Why, the idea is preposterous."

"But how can we know for sure?"

"Tristan. Even if we found out, you still can't have her."

"What if I wait until the end of the summer? Would you be more accommodating then?"

"No."

"Gaston." Tristan stomped his foot on the ground like a twelve-year-old.

"I'll tell you what. When our party comes to a close, if she has shown any interest towards you, you can proceed to woo her." Tristan drew an excited breath, but Gaston cut him off. "But not until she's out from underneath my roof, understood?"

He deflated some. "Very well. But how will we know for sure she isn't interested in her apprentice?"

Silence invaded the room like a thick mist. After a few frozen moments passed, Hector spoke up. "We should devise an amusement for her. Then I'm sure we can get at least some of our questions answered."

"I'm not so sure this is a good idea." Gaston frowned.

"I promise it will be done with the utmost delicacy."

"Make sure it is as you say or I'll have her slice you up and boil your bones."

Chapter Eight

Dawn had yet to break when Rory finished replacing and rearranging the items in the pantry. Although he was already exhausted, he knew that Ginny had given herself a few hours of extra sleep last night. A well-deserved bonus for her new-found status.

At the completion of the pantry reformation, Madame Simone fed both of them and sent them on their way to the market, one coach for the chef and her assistant, and a wagon for the purchased goods.

"I don't think she'll have any problems handling ham and eggs for the morning meal," Ginny commented to him along the way. "And it's lucky that the entire Leroux party will be away for luncheon."

"She's very competent. You are fortunate she stayed."

"I agree. But I must add how thankful I am that you're here, even though I originally protested your tagging along."

Ginny patted his hand, which rested on the seat between them, but before she could pull away, Rory withdrew his hand from beneath hers, only to switch their positions. His fingers closed gently over her cotton-encased digits. "I confess. I came for a totally different reason. I thought you needed protection, and here you are, taking me under your wing."

Her laughter tinkled like faery bells in the small compartment. "I've learnt a lot in the last twelve years."

Rory couldn't allow himself to remember the magical time when they'd first met, not now, not when he felt they were drawing closer to each other. He cleared his throat of the emotions welling up within him. "Tell me about Wellesley."

"Wellesley was..." She drew in a deep breath. "Lonely."

"How so?"

"All the other girls had come from society families. I came from an obscure mining camp." She waved a hand. "And that shoot-out next to Fly's didn't help matters either. Some of the more affluent girls enquired if one had to have killed a man in order to move to Tombstone."

"Imbeciles," he murmured with disgust.

"Ah, well." She chuckled. "I had my books, agreeable company on a cold winter's night."

Rory felt for her. He couldn't imagine not having someone to talk to. Even when Ace left to pursue his gambling career, Rory had still had dozens of friends in and around the plantation.

She grinned. "No need to look at me as if I were orphaned at a young age. I'm glad I spent the time alone. I had some soul-searching to do, after all."

"I'm sorry you went through that by yourself."

Ginny shrugged. "Without the journey through the fiery ovens, one isn't likely to transform, are they?"

"Although the prospect never seems pleasant at the time."

Her smile widened. "You have me there."

When the carriage pulled up to the markets, Rory breathed a sigh of relief that he'd been able to keep the conversation light and constant. He handed her down and together they faced their fate. It promised to be a sunny day, which mirrored his disposition perfectly. He was abroad with a beautiful woman, and they were enjoying themselves.

"I hear that to live through a French market and come out on top, one must possess a will of iron," she murmured to him.

"I defy anyone to cross Chef Clark."

He watched through the corner of his eye the way she looked at him. He'd never felt the hero until this very moment.

"Or her assistant."

His heart swelled with pride.

The very first merchant Virginia spoke with, after he assessed that she was an American, offered her an absurdly high price for beef sirloin.

"Monsieur, that is unacceptable." She spoke in his native French. "If you insist on that price, you'd better offer me twice the beef."

"Mademoiselle, this is not a charity house," the haughty butcher boasted.

"No, but neither is this a cut from the king's own cattle. I will be back in two hours and I expect twice the beef, along with three pounds *filet de bœuf*. And for the pains I suffered at your pretentiousness, you'll throw in four of your heartiest pre-plucked chickens, the lot of it packed in ice—a mixture of chippings and half blocks will do, or I will take my business to your competitor across the way."

He chuckled nervously. "No, no. That will not be necessary. We will have your order ready, you have my word."

Virginia nodded, turned on her heel and headed for the dairy merchants.

"What happened?" Rory asked. "I don't speak nearly as much French as you do."

"I just made a deal for two spectacular cuts of beef, demanded chicken as well, a fantastic price for all items and free ice to boot." She didn't mean for her tone to be smug, but she'd moved through the motions taught to her at school as if she'd invented dickering.

He murmured next to her ear, "Did I mention that you are amazing?"

She felt his hand at the small of her back and it sent shivers over her skin. He'd always know just the right things to say and do to bring out the tigress in her. Virginia admitted to herself that she'd missed him this way, missed his utterly male essence so close to her body, her soul. His strong support made her feel she could do anything. He treated her with respect, letting her take the lead in this outlandish venture. Yet he still used a gentle hand and, in a strange way, it made her feel fragile and feminine. His presence in France was becoming more and more of a comfort to her with every passing day.

And all his praise did wonders for her confidence. Now her only task, and perhaps the hardest part, was to hold the societal rules of courtship Beatrice had taught her close to her heart and not leap into Rory's arms the first chance she got.

The dairy and grain merchants, although they spoke English, weren't pushovers as the butcher had been. They both complained that she had to pay for the man-hours it took to churn the butter, skim the cream, age the cheese and grind the flour. However, Rory must have caught on to her technique for bartering. He'd negotiated with the half-dozen English-speaking merchants more than fair prices for the best they had, as if he'd been in attendance during her market training. Had there been an award given out for champion of the day, Rory would have won.

After purchasing the ingredients for Monsieur Leroux's sweet tooth, they passed by the floral and herbalist merchant tables. Virginia bought bushels of basil, sage, and coriander, a jar of imported vanilla beans from the West Indies, then negotiated for three ounces each of the freshest dill and rosemary.

Satisfied with the results so far, she turned to convey her thoughts to Rory.

He stood behind her poised to pin a beautiful gardenia to her bonnet. "For me?"

"Oh, drat. I was hoping to surprise you."

"What a lovely thought. Thank you." She tilted her head towards him.

When he finished, she took a step back. "How do I look?" She batted her eyelashes coquettishly.

Rory closed the distance between them. "Like a dream," he murmured and reached out to draw his fingertip from her throat to the tip of her chin.

His touch left a trail of delight across her skin and she became lost in the blue pools of his eyes. *Easy, girl,* she warned herself. *It's a flower, not a proposal.*

Providentially, he broke the spell. "What else do we have on our list?"

She drew in a shuddering breath and retrieved Madame Simone's list from the palm of her glove. Composing herself, she scanned the piece of paper.

"Just the produce is left. But I'm a bit hungry. Perhaps we could share a baguette and some cheese?"

He nodded and presented his elbow to her. "Shall we, then?"

Virginia's fingers slipped into the warm crook of his arm and they promenaded towards their destination.

As they casually strolled amongst the vendors, Rory knew it was vital that he keep mute his deep admiration towards Ginny if he was going to win her. The day had to be perfectly orchestrated to mirror his ardour, and at the same time, replant the seeds in her heart that he did in fact care for her.

"You know so much about food, and it seems I only know how to consume it."

Ginny's bright laughter floated above the crowd and seemed to excite the birds as they twittered in response. "It's not all that hard once you immerse yourself."

"As in diving head-first into a fountain of chocolate sauce?"

Another point for Rory. He was quite confident that each bout of giggles Ginny poured forth assisted his cause.

"No, silly, I mean in study."

"Oh, I see. So what drew you in originally?"

She smiled as if recalling a happy memory. "Back in Tombstone when Beatrice used to cook for the miners, she would let me stir the stew. I loved the fact that every Sunday, the stew was an entirely different creation. Once time it would be chicken, the next rabbit, we'd even gain a decent cut of beef once in a while. I was always intrigued that such diverse combinations of herbs and vegetables, along with the meat, could vary so. I mean, it was basically water, salt and some kind of meat. What in the world could cause such variations on your tongue?"

Rory swallowed. She was making his mouth water in more ways than one. "I see. So what was the first sort of food that intrigued you in school?"

"Without a doubt, bread."

"Bread? Something so simple?"

She stopped and faced him. "Rory. Have you ever had bread directly from the oven when it is so hot the butter melts the instant it touches it?" A sort of desire had sprung up in her gaze and Rory watched her lick her lips. She started forward again. "Bread is anything but simple. Have you any idea how many different kinds of bread there are in the world?"

"I suppose I don't."

"We'd be here all day if I were to launch into a lecture on the different grains, yeasts, kneading and rising processes. Then you have your flatbread varieties."

"But how does one know which one is good without tasting it?"

"Well, obviously, if you aren't enticed by the smell, it's likely you won't enjoy the taste." Ginny pulled him over to a bread vendor. "Here." She quickly stripped off her gloves and picked up a loaf of brownish bread with what looked like tiny seeds trapped inside the crust and held it under his nose for him to smell.

"Ew, I don't like that."

"This is rye bread. It's very popular in some regions owing to the fact that this bread lasts longer upon the shelf than any other."

"Can't imagine what it smells like towards the end of its time," Rory murmured so that the baker didn't hear.

She grinned and replaced the loaf only to choose another. "This is my favourite. French, of course, crusty on the outside but oh, so soft on the inside. Listen." Gently, she pressed the crust of the bread and it made a crackling sound. "Oh, don't you just want to slather on the butter an inch thick and sink your teeth into it?"

"Mmm." All of a sudden, Rory felt as if he hadn't eaten in weeks. He waved and gained the baker's attention. "We'll take this one."

He paid and accepted their purchase while Ginny slid her gloves on.

"Now, show me where the cheese and butter are before I devour this entire loaf by itself."

She laughed. "Oh, Rory." She took the bread from him and slipped her free hand into the crook of his elbow. "I'm going to make you wait until we have sweet, creamy butter and a hunk of well-aged cheddar."

"I don't think I can make it back to the dairy vendors," he groaned.

"Nonsense. A big strong man like you? Now come on."

Ginny steered him back towards the centre of the market.

Chapter Nine

Virginia supervised as Rory and their drivers loaded the wagon with the day's purchases. She was set for at least a week with meals, not to mention a few new additions to the pantry.

Having ordered the wagon to make for the Château Leroux with all haste, due to the iced foods, Rory handed her in and they both sighed when the carriage lurched forward.

"Well, Chef Clark, it seems we've conquered France."

"At least the markets. You were brilliant."

"I learned from the best."

"Smooth-talker." She giggled. "Is this flattery some of the Southern charm you learned from your Aunt Iris?"

He chuckled. "So the truth is flattery, now?"

"Offered up from a devil like you? Most likely," she taunted.

"And now I'm a devil?" he asked, feigning shock and sliding closer to her on the seat.

Virginia peered at him through slitted eyes. "I fear you Hughsons must have spirited away with a piece of the Blarney Stone before you arrived on our home shores."

Rory laughed. "My father may have, but Ace and I were born in the States."

She sobered some, and watched as he followed her lead. They sat in companionable silence for a little while when Virginia voiced a topic she'd been curious about for many years.

"Tell me, did your Aunt Iris come over from Ireland with your father?"

"Yes, they crossed the Atlantic just after he finished school. She'd wanted to go for many years, but apparently, grandfather wouldn't allow it until her brother was of age. They settled in Charleston where he worked in a warehouse and my aunt waited tables."

"And that's where he met your mother?"

"Yes." He grinned. "The daughter of the boss is usually off limits, but she couldn't resist the Hughson charm."

Virginia skittered her gaze across the ceiling of the carriage. "Yes, well…"

"And how do you know so much about us Hughsons?"

She felt heat roll up her neck to her cheeks. "I've kept tabs on you over the years via Beatrice and Luke's letters."

"You little sneak." He winked.

"Tell me about what you did for your aunt."

"Oh, just your generalities, I suppose. I escorted her to teas and cotillions, and helped her receive her guests, polished her favourite silver tea service once a week." He grinned, but his eyes held a far-away look.

"She wanted me to marry one of the society girls there, but I wasn't interested in any of them."

"I'll bet you were highly sought after."

He shrugged. "I didn't notice, really."

"You are being modest."

"Modest? Me?"

Virginia chuckled.

"Truly, what have I to offer a woman?"

"Are you fishing for compliments, now?"

"What? Of course not."

"M-hm. Sure you're not."

"You're a feisty little bit today, aren't you?"

Rory reached out and took her by the waist and Ginny squealed with delight. "Unhand me, fiend!" she teased.

"Never!" His fingers played along the sides of her corset like a piano. She couldn't truly feel it beneath her stays, but the action alone sent a strange giddiness through her.

After her fit of giggles he ceased his play. She caught her breath and at once, their eyes met, far more serious than a moment ago.

"This reminds me of our little trip to Tucson," Rory murmured.

Virginia nodded. "You must forgive me for the lapse in my moral conduct." She looked away.

"There's no need to apologise." With a knuckle beneath her chin he brought her focus back to his face. "We were younger then," he whispered.

"And now?"

"Now…" He drew so close she could feel the heat of him.

By their own volition, her eyes closed and, as she knew they would, his lips touched hers.

Her lips felt like heaven against his and tasted just as pure. "My Ginny," he couldn't help but whisper against her mouth. It was exactly as he remembered. His head filled with her scent. The softness of her skin drove him to the brink of insanity. He hadn't lied when he told her that he'd not been interested in any of the girls his aunt had introduced him to. All he could think about for years was Ginny, his sweet desert blossom.

And now here they were, her body straining to get closer to his on the seat of a damn carriage, just like before. She deserved better, and tonight he'd give it to her.

All too soon the carriage came to a stop. Ginny jumped away from him as if he'd burned her. She slid the back of a gloved hand across her kiss-swollen lips, removing the glossiness of their shared intimacy.

"I shouldn't have let this happen." She fled the carriage before he could recover.

Her hasty flight from the cab assisted in cooling his blatant desire. He exited and strode directly into the kitchen to take up a serious conversation with Ginny, but she was already involved in placing the new items into cold storage.

* * * *

Ginny had outdone herself for dinner. She'd wrapped the fillets in bacon and roasted them, catching the drippings into a pan where she added diced mushrooms and thickened the mixture with a bit of cornflour. The potatoes were whipped with plenty of butter and garlic, the plates were garnished with asparagus tips, and she included a chilled mixed green salad on the side with a creamy lemon-coriander dressing. She served it all at once—American style, she'd told the Leroux party—but saved her prize sweet cheese pastries for dessert.

Dinner that night could very well have been categorised as a masterpiece and she'd done it practically all by herself. She'd given Madame Simone the rest of the night off. After receiving high praise from her employer, she retired for the evening, having left instructions with her staff for the morning.

Rory helped finish up the dishes, and readied a few items for breakfast. Then, when everyone in the kitchen's attention turned elsewhere, he crept up the stairs to Ginny's room.

He rapped a knuckle upon her door.

No answer.

He tried again, a bit harder this time.

Still no answer.

Emboldened by her reaction to his kiss on the way to the château from the markets, Rory grasped the knob and let himself into the room. The curtains were drawn over the window, and the total darkness made it impossible to see. While listening to Ginny's steady breathing, his eyes adjusted to the lack of light. He stepped over to the bed. It was difficult to discern between the sheets and her nightgown, but in all the time he'd stood there, she hadn't moved, save for her breathing.

Obsessed, body and soul from want of her, Rory stifled a sigh. Concentrating on things in the kitchen had been near impossible because she'd flittered about the room, leaving her scent to mingle with the delectable food smells in the air. As much as he craved her like a starving man, she deserved to sleep after everything she'd accomplished today. He turned and left the room.

"Another time, perhaps," he whispered, not expecting a reply.

Back in his room, Rory found sleep to be as elusive as a live, greased piglet. The bed beneath him felt as if it stood next to the ovens. He kicked off his sheets, threw off his night shirt and lay there naked as a plucked game hen.

And all he could think about was his Ginny.

She'd been so brave in the market place, handling herself like a professional with those haughty vendors...how could he not admire her? Then, even after they had that intense eye to eye moment on the way home, and he'd kissed her, she still marched into that kitchen to delegate orders and get her own hands dirty along with the rest of the staff.

He yawned.

He could see her now, approaching the chopping block in the centre of all the goings on, with her arms folded across her chest, inspecting how Rory had cleaned and sorted the vegetables and herbs they'd purchased...

"You've done a good job, Mr Hughson." She picked up a *handful of coriander and shook off the droplets of water that seemed to cool the very air around him. "These can be dried a bit more, though. Once the excess water has been removed, they can be stored. I would like half hanging in the cold storage and half hanging in the pantry, is that clear?"*

He looked at her but was unable to respond. He resisted the urge to reach out and cup her cheek in his hand.

"I said, is that clear?"

Rory wanted to nod, but still he couldn't move.

"Do you understand me?" She took a step forward, her body pressed into his. "What's wrong with you?"

Finally, his limbs broke free of the peculiar debilitation. He took Ginny by the waist and hoisted her onto the chopping block, amongst the sweet smelling herbs.

Everything around them seemed to dissolve, including the staff. Rory looked down and both he and Ginny's clothes had vanished. Suddenly, there she was, his little seductress from the ride to Tucson.

"God, Ginny. How I want you."

She merely smiled her answer. And it was unmistakably a 'yes.'

She lay back, and Rory spread her thighs apart. He lapped at her pussy with his tongue. The sweetest cream flowed from her and he feasted on the delicacy. He knew that it ran down the sides of his mouth, but didn't dare attempt to wipe it away. He heard her moan and felt the twitching of her clit between his lips. She was coming. God, how he'd dreamt about making her come. Before she recovered from her crisis, he climbed up and slid his iron hard cock into her hot, velvety cunt. He rocked his hips against hers and she called his name over and over again.

He needed to come so badly. His muscles strained to reach his goal and he plunged deeper, listening to her cry out his name.

Something was not right. He'd made her orgasm, but the more he strove, his end seemed to be elusive, out of reach. Fuck he would explode soon.

Panting heavily, Rory sat up in bed, his sheet wrapped about his waist, his penis swollen and pressed against his belly. He wiped the sweat from his brow with the back of his hand.

Shit. *A dream, only a dream.* He attempted to convince himself.

He shook off the disorienting fog and went to the wash basin. With both hands he scooped up the water and doused his face and chest with it. Standing there, he looked down at the trouble maker between his legs.

"Aren't you supposed to be on my side? How many times are you going to put me in jeopardy?" He thought about the many faceless southern gals who'd enticed him into clandestine places, brought him to the brink, and instead of listening to his warnings that they should stop, they refused, coaxing him with flattery and feathery touches, saying that they wanted him to make love to them. None of the girls had been virgins, they'd only feigned the status. He was amazed that they had gotten away with such frequent indiscretions.

Rory knew that there was only one way he could get rid of the nagging stiffness between his legs. He took hold of his cock and his thoughts drifted back to his dream…back to Ginny's sweet, creamy pussy.

* * * *

Two weeks later, Monsieur Leroux took a tour of his newly reformed kitchen. He'd been curious as to the changes Virginia had made since Chef August's hasty retreat.

"Most impressive, Mademoiselle. You have reinvented the pantry."

"*Merci*, but I wouldn't go that far, Monsieur."

"I would bet good coin that our architect, Monsieur Guimard, would be interested in your thoughts on the perfect kitchen." He chuckled. "And you seem to have a bit more energy lately. Could it be that you are enjoying yourself?"

"How could I not? You have such a beautiful home, and this kitchen is a dream to work in. Tell Monsieur Guimard he would be hard pressed to improve upon its perfection." She smiled. "You have a wonderful staff here. Trust me, Monsieur, I want for nothing."

"There is one thing you lack, if I may say so."

"Really?" She couldn't be more certain that nothing could be farther from the truth.

"Amusement, Mademoiselle."

She shook her head. "No, no. I'm quite content, I assure —"

"Allow me to invite you to sit with us tonight."

Virginia searched for an excuse to bow out of his generous offer, but couldn't come up with anything that wouldn't offend him or make her seem prudish.

"Leave one of your staff in charge of the kitchen and enjoy a bit of frivolity."

"Truly, I could not do such a —"

"Now, I insist. Besides, my guests are becoming bored with only my face to look upon." He grinned slyly at his own remark, then continued. "I also know that Antonio wishes to ask you to sit for him." Gaston winked at her.

Had her head not been so fuzzy from the frenzy that was the kitchen, she might have come up with an excuse. She smiled amicably and nodded. "Very well, but not until the dishes are cleared. I couldn't completely abandon my staff, you know."

"*Bon*, then it's settled. I will see you tonight, but don't be late or I'll send Tristan in to fetch you. I think he dotes on you, Mademoiselle," he said with another wink.

* * * *

"Rory, it's just for a little while. I'm quite sure Monsieur Leroux will allow no harm to come to me."

"Then I will accompany you." Had she no idea about what went through men's heads when a desirable, vulnerable woman was tossed into the mix?

"For more reasons than I can name, you cannot do that."

Ginny's vague answer was entirely unacceptable. "Come now, you must be able to present a valid argument. I challenge you to name just one viable reason."

Her gaze dropped to the floor for a moment, then she stared him directly in the eyes. "You. Weren't. Invited."

Rory opened his mouth to protest, but she had him there. "Blast and damnation," he muttered.

Ginny chuckled. "Now now, there's no need for foul language." She turned on her heel and headed out of the door.

"Where are you off to?" he called after the headstrong woman.

"To fetch a few more bottles of wine for the evening meal. Don't worry, I shan't be accosted in the wine cellar, either."

Rory crossed his arms over his chest. "I swear if she's more than twenty minutes with those rogues tonight, I'll go in and fetch her myself."

Chapter Ten

A server set the last of the dessert dishes into the sink. Up to his elbows in dishwater, Rory reached for the next plate.

Virginia quickly untied her apron and set it upon a shelf. She smoothed her hair into place and did the same for the skirt of her dress. She'd strode through the doors and down the hall to Monsieur Leroux's parlour before Rory had noticed she'd gone.

Upon entering the cigar smoke-filled room, she was greeted by the party, except for Monsieur Leroux, who seemed to be asleep on a divan in the corner.

The novelist, the one Monsieur Leroux teased her about having a crush on her, reached out his hand and drew her into the centre of the room. "Ah, here is our angel, *mes amis*."

Her cheeks heated, but what did she expect? "Monsieurs, I am no angel." To her surprise, they laughed at her mundane response.

"Good," the painter replied, a droll tone colouring his voice. "That is how I like a woman, as far from an angel as possible."

They chuckled again and Virginia could have kicked herself in the backside for not seeing that one coming. "That's not exactly what I meant." She glanced around at the men, who seemed to be closing in on her. "Gentlemen, have you enough cigars? Enough to drink?"

A glass of well-aged cabernet sauvignon pressed into her hand and she grasped it. "Every good artist knows that inspiration is found in the oddest of places."

"So sayeth the architect," Antonio pointed out.

"Monsieur? I don't understand," Virginia murmured, glancing down at her drink.

The novelist grinned. "I think what Monsieur Guimard is trying to convey is that at the bottom of this glass you will find you've gained an even more approachable disposition."

"I..."

"Drink up, Mademoiselle, before it loses its bouquet." Tristan assisted the glass to her lips and tipped the bottom up.

Virginia gulped the red wine down with his help, not wishing to offend him. They cheered when the glass emptied. She patted her lips dry with the back of her hand.

"Antonio," Tristan asked the painter. "What was that game you were telling us about? I think now would be a better time than any to teach it to us."

"*Oui*. Mademoiselle, would you indulge us in a little guessing game?"

The innocuous game intrigued her. "Of course. What could be more amusing than a guessing game?"

With that, Tristan untied his cravat bow and handed it to Antonio.

"Now." Antonio placed himself behind Virginia. "I am going to cover your eyes. You will be guessing the who's, what's and where's."

The blindfold slipped over her face before she could enquire further.

Oh, dear.

Virginia gasped slightly when two strong hands captured her by the waist. Tristan's voice chuckled closer to her ear than a moment before.

The very air reeked of alcohol fumes—whisky, cognac, red wine, all mingled together, blowing hot on her face and neck. If the cloud of spirits reached an open flame, they'd all combust.

The moment Antonio finished his knot, he ordered Virginia to be spun around eight times. By the fourth spin, disorientation overtook her and the tiny glass of wine she'd had wasn't helping a bit.

When the spinning finally stopped, she stumbled forward, but not before she was caught by at least two sets of hands. "Thank you," she murmured.

Another pair of hands settled upon her shoulders, warm, comforting, kneading the tired muscles there. "Now, Mademoiselle," an indistinct male voice whispered. "Can you guess who is speaking to you now?"

The voice sent a sensual tremor through her. Feather-light fingers crept their way up her back, ending at the nape of her neck, tickling the hair there.

"Um..." Virginia thought for a moment while the goose bumps passed over her skin. "The man with the French accent?"

Her fellow game players chuckled all around her.

"Is she not beautiful?" one of them murmured just loud enough for her to hear.

"She would make a lovely model."

"Go on, ask her to sit for you."

"Later. Right now I want to play."

Before she could raise a protest to the whispered words that to her teetered on the edge of wicked, someone lifted her hand in the air.

"Who has your hand, Mademoiselle?"

"I... I don't..."

"And your other hand?" Insistent fingers enfolded her digits and lifted her hand into the air.

Virginia imagined she looked pretty silly right about now when a draft seeped up beneath her skirts. She tensed and felt the ground sway like a ship's deck.

"Allow her to sit down and regain her bearings."

She was ushered a few steps forward and they bid her to sit. The cushion was unstable — lumpy at best when she realised she'd not been led to her own seat, but to someone's lap.

"Set her feet upon the ottoman."

Warm hands encircled her ankles then, setting her legs out straight, they came to rest on what felt suspiciously like another pair of legs.

The warning bells didn't sound in her head until the hands that were paddling her ankles slid to her knees. Virginia drew in a breath to protest when she was at once unceremoniously dumped upon the ground. The blindfold was snatched from her eyes, and there before her stood Rory. And Heavens, but he was angry, like a rattlesnake who'd been teased with a stick. His eyes blazed blue fire and his face was red as a sunburn. She could only wish that the colour of his skin was a result of having just come from working up to his elbows in hot dish water, but she knew differently.

"What the Hell is going on here?" He reached out and helped her to stand. She released him and rubbed her damp palms together.

"Nothing untoward, I assure you, Monsieur," Tristan pleaded with upturned hands and a crooked smile.

"Oh, I see. Having one's skirts shoved up to her thighs is 'nothing untoward' in your book?"

"Come now, Monsieur, we were only playing a little game—"

"Hang you and your games, Frenchie."

"Rory!" Virginia choked out.

"Do not attempt to defend them," Rory barked at her. "I know what I saw." He glanced around at the four men. "Where is Leroux?" he ordered.

"He's asleep on the divan," Virginia pointed out.

Rory harrumphed. "You mean passed out, don't you? Come on." He took Virginia by the hand. "We are leaving."

Amid the male protests, Virginia's were the loudest. "Leaving?" She sputtered as he drew her into the hall and through the kitchen.

Rory slammed the door to her room after they'd entered. To Virginia, he looked quite like a terribly annoyed big brother. "Rory, don't be too upset. It was harmless fun, I assure you."

"And just how far would you have allowed it to go, may I ask?"

"I'm certain they wouldn't have—"

"Like Hell!" he bellowed. "You were blindfolded, and they were practically sitting on you!"

"To be precise, I was sitting on them."

"This is not how a lady behaves, let alone a Chef!"

That stung. "I can take care of myself, Rory."

"You have not yet proven you can do so."

"You've not yet given me the chance," she shot back.

Rory ran both hands through the top of his hair. "It was a damn good thing I was there to put a stop to it all."

"Oh, Rory—"

"Pack your things. We are leaving in the morning."

"No! I want to make my way in this world, and I'm not going to let a little flirting stop me!"

"Is that what you call that...that *display* out there?"

"Look, I know you don't understand, but I need to prove myself and what better place than the male-dominated culinary arts?"

"And is allowing your employer to treat you like a common tart part of the bargain?"

Virginia was so appalled her jaw dropped open. "How dare you say such a thing?"

Rory gritted his teeth. "Regardless, we depart for home tomorrow."

Unmoved by his anger, she retorted, "No. I am going to stay and finish this job."

"I'm not leaving without you—"

"That suits me just fine. We both stay and together see this thing through to the end."

She watched his chest rise and fell with every irritated breath.

"We'll see about that," he ground out.

Then next thing she knew she stood alone in her room.

"Men can be so infuriating!" She stamped her foot on the wood floor.

"Women can be so infuriating!" Rory huffed as he paced in his small room. "My God, they may as well have been disrobing her, in fact, that's exactly what those rogues were doing!"

So astonished, not to mention enraged, that Ginny wouldn't even admit she was in danger, Rory could have fried an egg on top of his head. If he hadn't been there…he didn't even want to know what would have become of her. Damnation, had she no idea what unscrupulous men were capable of?

What the Hell was so important that she needed to endure such humiliation? He'd said it from the beginning and he'd say it now, this trip to France had been the worst idea since barbers began bleeding sick people.

Who knew what else those artist bastards would try to orchestrate?

Rory strode over to his door and opened it a crack. Then he pushed his bed towards the door so that he could keep watch on Ginny's door all night long. One of those drunken Frenchies might decide she was a midnight snack and wander up to her room.

He sat down on his bed and focused on her door.

Ginny was his, damn it.

His.

Chapter Eleven

"And so, we shall depart for England this afternoon."

Virginia heard Rory make his announcement just before she burst into Monsieur Leroux's study. "I am not going anywhere, Monsieur," she said as calmly as possible. "I don't care what Mr Hughson does, but I'm staying."

"No, you're not."

"Oh, yes I am."

Monsieur Leroux, still in his green velvet brocade dressing robe, pressed his fingers to his temples. "Please. This is unnecessary."

Virginia lowered her voice. She'd heard that if one overindulged, they might be inclined to headaches. "Forgive me, Monsieur," she whispered contritely.

"If you would both sit, I can try and tell you what my drunken friends—"

"There is nothing to explain. We are leaving and that is final," Rory said with far less sensitivity than Virginia.

She felt panic rise in her throat at Rory's words. She wasn't about to toss everything out of the window over this silly matter. Quickly she sat before her assistant could protest further.

"Monsieur?" Her employer kindly offered Rory a seat with tilt of his head toward the matching leather chair next to Virginia's.

Rory declined and crossed his arms over his chest. If his disposition proved as unmovable as his stance, she had a fight ahead of her.

"Earlier this morning, much to my discomfort, my guests filed into my room to tell me what went on last night while I was...indisposed."

Rory opened his mouth to comment but stopped when Virginia cleared her throat, tossing the action in his direction as best she could.

Monsieur Leroux continued, "They wish to express their regret. They realise now that unattached men, wine and a beautiful woman should be considered mixed company."

"Thank you, Monsieur, I accept their apology."

"I, however, do not," Rory insisted.

"Monsieur Hughson, what can I do to make it up to you and Mademoiselle Clark?"

Rory eyed her employer. "Put an end to this party and send Miss Clark home."

"No, don't, Monsieur. I'm sure we can come to a compromise. Perhaps we could find someone to take over the position of head —"

"Ginny, if you felt you were unable to dig up another kitchen staff, I doubt Leroux could produce another Head Chef."

"And would this idea ease your mind, Monsieur Hughson?" Leroux asked.

She could feel the wheels of Rory's mind churning from where she stood. "Yes, I believe it would. Although I can't see it happening."

"Why not? I know a few people around here, as you may well guess."

"Because I don't think you could come up with someone by, say, sundown."

"Rory, that's too soon, it's not fair!" she demanded in Monsieur Leroux's defence, but apparently, no one was listening.

"Are those your terms, Monsieur Hughson?"

"They are."

Virginia sunk deeper into her chair at Rory's smug answer.

Monsieur Leroux nodded. "Done. Now, what sort of breakfast can me and my guests expect this morning?"

Before Virginia could speak, Rory jumped in. "Runny eggs and greasy sausage."

Monsieur Leroux clapped a hand over his mouth and fled the room.

"Rory!" Virginia scolded the tittering twit.

* * * *

"Are you mad? The way you'd originally presented last night's little game to me was far less innocent than what you claimed! I had a visit early this morning from Mademoiselle Clark's apprentice." Gaston pressed his index fingers to his temples, holding his skull together.

"Come now, the boy must have exaggerated. We did nothing—"

"No, Hector. Whatever you have to say I don't want to hear. You offended Mademoiselle Clark."

"All right. You don't have to shout." Hector looked in the same state as Gaston felt.

"Actually, it was her assistant who raised the affront. Mademoiselle Clark was—"

"Tristan. I warned you to wait until the end of summer. Your impatience coupled with your unmanageable lust is more trouble than I want. And now if I don't find another chef by sundown, Mademoiselle Clark is going to leave."

"What?" Antonio whispered painfully from his sunken position in a nearby chair. "She wouldn't."

"It seems her apprentice insists on it."

"Is he more her chaperone than her assistant?"

"I told you he loves her, Tristan. I should have made a wager. I could be a rich man right now."

"Shut up, Antonio—"

"Stop it, all of you. Don't you have better things to occupy yourselves with than the help? We should be creating, inventing, bringing to the world something unique and all you can do is cause trouble." His guests went quiet, thank God, for his head could take no more.

"We'll apologise," one of them murmured.

"Yes, you will, to her apprentice as well if the situation presents itself. Afterwards you will leave Mademoiselle Clark alone for the rest of the summer."

Gaston was satisfied with their non-verbal agreement. "This only solves part of the problem. I must find a new chef before I am forced to send all of you home." He sighed. "Now out. I have some letter-writing to do."

* * * *

It was easy to forgive Rory and almost forget his demands when the duties of chef called on Virginia. The day had been a whirl of activity in the kitchen. She'd served a late, rather dry breakfast to Monsieur Leroux and his recovering guests, and endured profuse apologies in both French and English. They'd promised her nothing so suspicious would ever happen again and even offered to sponsor her in an upcoming pastry competition, which she waved off, telling them the kind gesture was unnecessary.

She proposed a proper high tea at four o'clock and they accepted graciously.

"That's it. Tiny strokes, Rory. Pull in and out while gently squeezing." She instructed her assistant on the fine art of piping white icing onto the blue and green petit-fours she'd made for the tea. "Yes, just like that. Excellent." She chuckled. "Even I couldn't produce such perfection."

Rory grumbled. "It's not so hard once you get used to it."

"Wonderful. Now when you finish, please set the dish directly onto the bed of crushed ice in cold storage." She wheeled the cart into the dining room to set the table.

Monsieur Leroux's valet popped his head inside. "Please set the table for six. The Monsieur is expecting one more guest this afternoon."

* * * *

"Monsieur Emile Monet, allow me to introduce Mademoiselle Clark. She originates from the United States and has been cooking for me and my friends since the beginning of summer."

The tall, darkly handsome Frenchman took her hand in his and lifted her fingers to his lips. "I am honoured, Mademoiselle," he breathed across her skin, then placed a kiss upon her knuckles.

Oh, my. "Merci, Monsieur Monet." His fathomless black eyes and striking, classic features stirred Virginia's insides. Lord, but he was handsome.

"Please, call me Emile." He grinned and released her hand rather reluctantly, it seemed.

"Sit for with us for a moment, Mademoiselle," Monsieur Leroux asked.

"But Monsieur, the kitchen—"

"Come. I insist."

Emile offered her his seat, pulling over another chair for himself from the corner of the room. A thrill sifted through Virginia when he settled his seat very close to hers.

Emile rested his arm across the back of her chair which made concentrating on the conversation most difficult.

"Where did you grow up, Mademoiselle Clark?"

"Well, Monsieur Monet, I—"

"Please. Emile."

"Then I insist you call me Virginia."

"Done."

She smiled. "My formative years were spent in a little boomtown in the Arizona territory called Tombstone. I completed my education in New York, and then went to cooking school on the east coast as well. And you?"

"I was born in Spain, as my father is a *Général de Brigade* in the French Foreign Legion. My father and mother brought me up, following the Legion from country to country." He shrugged. "But when my education was complete, I didn't wish to join the corps with my father, so I came to France to seek out his side of the family."

"And you've been here ever since?"

"That is correct. I've lived here for fifteen years now. I have many friends and I love France. It is here I call home."

Virginia nodded in acknowledgement. She glanced around at the other men at the table. Aside from a few murmurings, Monsieur Leroux's party had for the most part, remained silent.

Tristan leant forward and addressed Virginia. "I can see, Mademoiselle, that I started off on the wrong foot with you. I should have talked about my parents first. Then perhaps you would have paid more attention to me."

Virginia had to raise her voice above the laughter. "I assure you, Monsieur Bernard, I have no intention of playing favourites with any of Monsieur Leroux's guests."

"Well, I'm glad to hear it," Monsieur Leroux said, his grin unashamed.

"I'm not." Tristan pouted.

Monsieur Leroux continued. "What I mean to say is, Monsieur Monet is not just a guest, but our new head chef, per my agreement with Monsieur Hughson. Do forgive the way in which I introduced you, Mademoiselle. I merely wanted to see if you would get on."

"I'm quite sure the Mademoiselle and I will get on famously."

Yes, getting along with Emile certainly won't be a problem. Virginia turned to find Emile smiling wolfishly into her eyes, simply devouring her. She grinned. Things were about to get interesting in the Leroux kitchen with such a man in charge.

Rory burst into the room with a bit more force than necessary. His gaze scanned the room and landed on Virginia. "I was curious as to what was taking you so long in here."

Monsieur Leroux chuckled. "Fear not, Monsieur Hughson, Mademoiselle Clark is not being accosted. You may rest assured of this from now on."

She watched as Rory's attention was drawn to Emile, who sat awfully close to her. Rory's eyes narrowed for an instant and he gave the man the once-over as one would a rival on the field of honour. Virginia doubted anyone else had noticed. The flash of jealousy she perceived extracted a feeling of feminine power that was foreign to her and, oddly enough, wasn't at all unpleasant.

Virginia stood. "Rory, this is our new head chef, Emile."

Emile inclined his head to Rory.

"Monsieur Emile," Rory said acknowledging him in return.

"No. It is Monsieur Monet."

Rory shot her a look which she knew conveyed his displeasure that she had used the man's first name. His scalding line of sight returned to Emile, his smile forced. The relationship between the two men would be precarious at best, Virginia mused with no small amount of dread.

Virginia refused to allow the moment to continue on its destructive path. She excused herself and Rory. However, before she could escape, Emile stopped her.

"Virginia, perhaps after supper you will give me a private tour of the kitchen?"

She smiled politely. "Of course."

Holding open the kitchen door for the servers, Rory looked at Virginia, his countenance stern, his voice more so. "This new chef is not to my liking."

Once the cart passed and the door separating the hall to the kitchen closed, Virginia continued the conversation. "Why ever not? You haven't even worked with him yet."

"First of all, he shouldn't have women under him."

Rory's statement stirred up all sorts of visions Virginia had to push from her mind. "I—I beg your pardon?"

"I mean, a woman—working under him."

Poor Rory. He was having a very difficult time expressing himself and Virginia couldn't help but be amused. She failed to stifle a childish giggle.

"I don't mean... That is to say..." He cleared his throat.

Still smiling, Virginia folded her arms and waited for Rory to clarify.

"I...I don't like the way he looks at you."

"And how is that?" She knew exactly what he meant. However, she happened to like the intensity of Emile's gaze and the way it made her heart skitter.

"As if...as if he's taking your clothes off with his eyes."

"Nonsense."

"I find it difficult to believe that you don't feel it, too."

Virginia shrugged. "I feel nothing of the kind." Even though she did, and quite frankly, enjoyed every moment she'd spent thus far under Emile's dark scrutiny.

Rory turned away and leaned a hip against the counter, folding his arms across his chest. "I'm not happy about the choice."

"Your happiness was not part of the bargain you struck with Monsieur Leroux. As I recall, you simply said, 'by sundown'."

"Regardless, I will be keeping a close eye on him—on both of you."

She'd won this round. Relief spread through her being like bread sopping up gravy. "Well"—Virginia grinned smugly—"that's what chaperones are for, after all."

* * * *

"We must go out of doors each time to get to the cold storage?" Emile asked as he held one of the storm doors open for Virginia.

"Yes, but it's not so bad," she said as they descended the half-flight of stairs. "In fact, it can be a refreshing reprieve from the kitchens, especially when all four ovens are working at the same time." At the bottom of the steps, she held the candle higher to light the narrow corridor. "To the left is the wine cellar and to the right is the cold storage."

"How well-stocked is the wine cellar?" He leaned a hand on the wall above her head.

Though she detected a twinkle in his eye, she ignored it. "Monsieur Leroux only houses the best wines here. His *Veuve Clicquot* is kept in cold storage in a special trunk."

"Ah, a man of very fine tastes indeed." He leaned in towards her.

She smiled. There was that look again, the look that sent her blood rushing through her body, and Rory into a rampage.

"Will you show me the wine cellar? You have me quite curious, Mademoiselle."

She handed him the candle holder and inserted an iron key, which was kept on a nail next to the door, into the lock.

He stepped in behind her and held the candle high. "A good-sized room," he murmured. "Tomorrow, see to it that a small table and two chairs are brought in from the kitchen and placed here in the centre."

"I shall." She nodded, not having any idea what it was for, but not wanting to question her superior.

"Now let us see the cold storage."

"You won't want furniture put in there, too, will you?"

She couldn't help but grin when Emile laughed.

* * * *

Madame Simone returned from the markets just after lunch and the entire kitchen staff assisted with putting away the new purchases. Everyone on staff could at any time fetch an item, so intimate were they with where things were kept. Emile had complimented Ginny on this, and said it made the kitchen run with an unparalleled efficiency.

Rory thought the new chef too familiar with Ginny, and it pricked at him something awful.

Supper that evening would be a very special event, or so Ginny had declared. Emile had created a menu merely by looking at the new arrivals from the market.

Again Rory thought the two were overly polite and accommodating to each other. Something was cooking in that suave Frenchman's mind, and Rory was afraid it was Ginny's goose.

"Flirting. That's what he's doing. Flirting with her," Rory had mumbled more than once that day. Was it too much to ask that all these smooth-talking Frenchmen keep to themselves?

Rory and Madame Simone spent the afternoon chopping celery, carrots and potatoes into inconceivably tiny cubes. Then they added seasoned breadcrumbs and a bit of chicken stock to moisten the mixture. Afterwards, Emile dismissed Madame Simone and had Rory holed up in the corner plucking, gutting and stuffing no less than a dozen Cornish game hens. The private tutors Aunt Iris had provided would surely take a switch to his hide for stooping so low.

Rory grumbled about the work, but was promptly shushed by Ginny as she put the finishing touches on her fancy pie crusts for the evening's dessert tarts.

"Tonight, Mademoiselle," Emile leaned over the counter and eyed Ginny like a python would a mouse, "I want you to join me for a wine tasting. I would like to educate you on what food goes with which wine in Monsieur Leroux's cellar."

"Thank you, Emile." She smiled at him, gazing into his eyes like some love-sick puppy, at least that was what it looked like to Rory. He gritted his teeth and jammed a handful of stuffing down the neck hole of a hen.

"Be sure to bring an appetite for luxury with you tonight."

"I am intrigued, Monsieur."

Had she just batted her eyelashes at him? Rory heard the bones of the bird in his hand crack.

"Meet me in the wine cellar at eleven o'clock."

"I'll be there."

Emile, looking irritatingly smug, left the kitchen via the back door.

"Be sure you spit."

Ginny turned to Rory. "I beg your pardon?"

"Spit. Don't swallow."

Her countenance went from amused to perplexed. "I still don't follow."

"Don't drink the wine. He'll get you drunk and who knows what he'll do with you then."

She glared at him. "What a study of human interest you are. I've never seen someone so envious of nothing before in my life."

Ginny slid the pies into an oven, then stomped up the stairs to her room.

Rory was tired. Tired of this nonsense and tired from working so hard. Tonight would yield many truths about this infatuation with Ginny. That was what it was, after all, right, an infatuation? No. It was more. Much more. The thought punched him in the stomach and he nearly doubled over.

Damn Emile and his snake-like charm. If the hen in his hands had had a neck, Rory would have wrung it.

Chapter Twelve

Virginia descended the stairs and crossed the kitchen. She felt Rory's gaze on her all the way from the sinks on the other side. So what if she'd changed out of her working dress and coiffed her hair? It was none of Rory's business what she did. She exited the kitchen via the back way and strode down the path. *If he wasn't so irksome. If he wasn't so nosey.* She sighed. *And if only he felt the same way I do about him.* Smoothing out the front of her sky-blue linen gown, she made her way through the storm doors and down the steps.

Candlelight seeped into the dim passage from the wine cellar and she approached with a pinch of trepidation and a dash of caution.

As she entered, Emile stood. "Virginia. Punctual as always."

The normally dank cellar glowed with warmth. Emile had placed empty bottles, which supported lit candles, in clever spots. The ivory wax dripped down the green glass giving them a quaint, old-world look. He'd swept the floor and draped dainty cobweb lace about the room. In the centre, the elaborately dressed table sat flanked by the two chairs that now sported cushions.

He held out his hand to her and she slipped her fingers into his warm palm. Emile drew her into the room and shut the cellar door behind them.

She hoped he couldn't sense her apprehension, as trivial as it was. "You've gone to some lengths, Monsieur, to conduct a wine tasting with a mere pastry chef."

He showed her to one of the chairs. "I wanted you to feel comfortable, not like you were being held captive in a dungeon."

Had Emile been the dungeon master it would've, at the very least, made things interesting. She almost laughed out loud at the thought. Rory would've had a thing or two to say about that. She smiled. "With you along for company, who could feel like a captive?"

Emile chuckled and snapped a linen napkin in the air with a flourish. He laid the cloth over his forearm and bowed, presenting the fare before them with an upturned palm.

On the table sat four open bottles of wine and a platter with various cheeses garnished with strawberries cut like flowers. On a small, smartly crafted table next to Emile were crystal wine glasses that sparkled in the dancing candlelight. He must have brought the beautifully carved drinking vessels from somewhere inside the house.

Emile plucked two of the glasses from the small table, expertly drizzled a heady red into each of them and set them before her. "Tell me, Mademoiselle, what do your tastes lean towards?"

His double entendre was delivered with the slightest grin and a definite twinkle in his eye. "Tastes,

Monsieur?" She refused to give him the satisfaction and knowledge that his magnetism intrigued her.

"Does your palate crave sweet treats or salty delicacies?"

She'd have to choose her words carefully lest she get caught in the fine web he cast. "Given the choice between confections or say, fresh-baked bread, I would gravitate toward the bread."

Victoria could tell by the slight pause that he was looking for another way under her skin.

"Then I think you would enjoy this pinot noir from Burgundy. With this particular label, you can detect a hint of cherry, as they integrate cherry trees along with the pinot meunier vines. Now, this is how I want you to experience the taste. First, close your eyes."

"Monsieur…" She'd played this game before and the results were less than permissible.

"Do not be afraid."

"I am not afraid, I assure you."

"Then close your eyes and open your mouth."

"What are you going to do?" she asked and peered at him. He had yet to win her trust, after all, and with what happened with Monsieur Leroux's other guests, she supposed she should attempt to be cautious.

Emile sighed and took his seat. "All right. We shall compromise."

This made her feel a thousand times better.

"Here." He reached over, plucked a small chunk of yellow cheese from the platter and fed it to her. "Just after you swallow, I want to you take a sip of your wine, shut your eyes and tell me what you taste." He pressed a glass into her hand.

With one last assessing glance, she did as he told her, feeling silly that she'd suspected him of indelicacies. This tasting that Emile had set up seemed harmless enough. And she wouldn't spit, either. It was rude for Rory to even suggest such a thing.

"Mmm."

"Tell me," he nearly whispered close to her ear.

Her eyes popped open and found him cosying up to her side, but not touching her. "The wine made the taste of the cheese come to life in my mouth!"

"And what a beautiful mouth you have."

Beautiful mouth? She couldn't help the giggle that escaped her lips. "What an odd thing to say."

"Not from where I sit, Mademoiselle."

Virginia had no idea how to react to his statement.

"Now I want you to compare this next wine with the first one." He removed her old glass, poured the next selection into a new glass and handed it to her.

She sipped. "Hm. Richer. Fuller. Is this an older bottle?"

"It is, however this Bordeaux is made from cabernet sauvignon grapes as opposed to the pinot. Any red wine will enhance well-flavoured meats and will do the same for them as what you experienced with the cheese." Emile tossed back the wine in front of him, then leaned his head towards hers. "Tell me, Mademoiselle, where do your friend Rory's tastes lie?"

* * * *

"A full hour." Rory prowled back and forth in his small room above stairs. "They've been down there a full hour." He growled, his irritation growing as each splinter of time passed. "The longest bloody hour of my life." During the last half of the seeming eternity, Rory had steeled himself against sneaking down and pressing his ear to the door, but now he was crawling out of his skin with apprehension. Waiting was obviously not his cup of tea.

Was she drunk right now, her inhibitions scattered to the wind? He knew well her passion and how it flowed like a river, even without the influence of spirits.

He gritted his teeth. *Is that cad, Emile taking advantage of Ginny at this very moment?*

Rory sat down at the foot of the bed and scraped his fingers through his hair. "Or am I just the biggest fool on God's green earth to be caring for someone who won't reciprocate my feelings?" he mumbled.

Regardless of whether he should be branded a fool or not, he had to know what was going on down there. Resolved to find out and stop the damnable voices in his head, he forged ahead. He crept down the smooth wooden servant's stairs, crossed the cold kitchen floor and slunk out of the back door.

Opening the storm doors without making a noise was much easier than Rory had imagined. Once he'd closed them and navigated the narrow stone steps that led to the hallway between the cold storage and the wine cellar, he found himself steeped in inky darkness. Rory held his breath, listening for a sound, any sound.

Moments passed. Nothing. He felt his way over to the wine cellar door and found the knob. Slowly he sank to his knees, anticipating the lurid scene he was about to witness through the keyhole, involving the woman he loved and another man.

Good God. He loved Virginia Clark!

Rory filled his lungs to capacity with air hoping to settle his beating pulse and chase away the rampant panic he felt in his heart. He peered into the hole with one eye.

Ginny and that damn rogue, Emile, had their heads together, all close and cosy-like. They seemed to be deep in conversation, whispering to each other. After a few exchanges, Ginny covered her mouth and giggled. They stood and Emile took her hand and kissed her knuckles.

Rory didn't know whether to be relieved Emile hadn't ravished Ginny or angry that the Frenchie had taken her to a private room and, from the looks of things, romanced her into his sinister circle.

"Let me clean this up, Emile. You've been so kind to do all this for me."

He released her and waved a hand in dismissal. "I won't hear of it. This is my doing and I shall undo it. You run along up to bed. Breakfast comes early, even in this enchanting château."

Ginny thanked Emile and turned towards the door.

Rory had only tripped twice on the way up the stairs, all the while praying Ginny hadn't heard his clumsy retreat.

Once he crossed the threshold of the kitchen, he slammed his toe as he hastily turned the corner to the stairs. "Damnation!" Rory grabbed his foot and jumped up and down for a moment. Had he originally thought to put on his shoes he'd be up in his room already. The servant's stairs were much harder to take while limping. He barely made it into the hallway to his door, when Ginny turned the corner.

"Oh," Ginny sounded as if he'd startled her. "What are you still doing up?"

He leaned casually against the wall. "You know, just...taking the air."

"It's after midnight. Rory, are you unwell?" she asked and approached him, motioning to set her palm to his forehead. Her hand landed before he could pull away. "Your skin is clammy."

Rory drew in a breath and exhaled on a laugh. "Nonsense. I'm fine."

"Your breathing is irregular, too. Are you sure you are all right?" Her hand went from his head to his heart. "And my goodness, but your heart is pounding something awful."

The intimate touch did nothing to calm his pulse so he changed the subject. "How was your wine tasting? You seem...sober."

Her hand fell to her side in a fist. "Sober and unmolested, if it's any of your business."

"I'm surprised, that's all."

"Surpri—" Indignation rang in her tone, choking off her words. A splash of anger served as a balm to her vocal cords. "Rory Hughson, you don't trust me, do you?" Her question was delivered as a statement.

"I don't trust *him*."

"That is not the issue," she hissed. "You. Don't. Trust. *Me*."

"I—"

"The answer should be a simple yes or no. Do you have it in you to dispense either of those words in reference to this situation?"

"It's not as simple as—"

"All right. I'm going to assume your answer is 'no.'" Rory had tried to cut in, but she continued her reprimand. "Regardless of my having proven myself this very night, from now on it's strictly business between you and me. My friends and I don't harbour trust issues." With that she flounced into her room and shut her door none too daintily.

Rory fell against the wall and exhaled. He'd mucked up his chance to tell Ginny how he really felt and now he'd have to find a way to wade through the thick fog in her head and tell, no, *show* her that he loved her. And he'd have to accomplish all this without allowing her to put herself at peril.

Damnation.

He'd rather clean and stuff a hundred game hens.

Chapter Thirteen

Rory lay awake in his bed staring at the ceiling. The last two weeks had not gone as planned. Not once did he find himself in the position to approach Ginny in a proper manner.

Tonight during clean-up, he'd witnessed Emile invite Ginny to a coffee tasting. They were to meet outside on the east veranda at seven in the morning. Leroux and the boys wouldn't return until supper from a visit to the village. Ha! The local whorehouse, more like. As long as they stayed far away from Ginny. He had enough on his hands with that snake Emile winding his way around Ginny's heart, Rory mused bitterly.

Emile had planned an entire early-morning meal around Italian coffee versus American, then they were to take their beverages into Leroux's study, where Emile would show Ginny a historical timeline of coffee popularity.

It was the most ridiculous ruse he'd ever heard of in his life.

If Rory could think up showy, trivial ways to get Ginny alone, would she fall for it? She certainly had done so with the smooth Frenchie, Emile.

Rory's only consolation was that for the first part of their little morning party, they'd be in plain sight, not locked in a tiny, candle-lit room. Well, at least until they shut themselves off together in Leroux's damn study.

He flopped onto his side. If he held his tongue, didn't make a single comment, didn't even glance their way, could he present it to Ginny later as evidence that he trusted her? He promised himself one peek through the library keyhole, and only for a second. Or two.

* * * *

Rory almost yelled in protest at the sight of Emile plaiting Ginny's hair. There was no mistaking the intimate action, even through the small keyhole. He calmed his breathing after a moment and took a second look just to make sure.

"You see, if you incorporate your hair from all sides, each in turn, you won't have one heavy tail tugging at your scalp all day long."

Ginny sighed. "Ah, you are right. It feels much better. Thank you, Emile."

"Now let me see you." He took her by the shoulders and turned her to face him. "Very becoming, Mademoiselle. You look good enough to eat."

That was it! Rory burst into the room and they turned in synchronisation to look at him. "Do you have everything you require?" Thank God his voice did not betray his seething emotions. "More sugar or cream, perhaps?" He smiled, hoping it appeared sincere.

Emile grinned at Rory, an odd sparkle in his eyes gleaming with what looked like mischievousness. Rory was sure that the bastard could feel his jealousy from across the room where he stood, too close to Ginny.

Ginny stole a glance at Emile, then turned to Rory. "I think we have everything we need, thank you."

Rory huffed out a pent-up breath. "Very well, then. Proceed with what you were doing. Not that I know what you were doing. That is to say, if you were doing anything. Anything at all." He bit down on his tongue to stop his babbling and hurried out of the door, shutting it behind him.

From the hallway, he heard Emile's deep voice mumble something. Ginny responded with her sensual tone, "Emile!" Then she giggled. Rory could hear nothing else from inside the library. He could have kicked himself in the seat of his trousers for turning into a bumbling fool in front of his adversary.

If that isn't true love then pixies aren't real.

The unspoken voice reminded him of something Aunt Iris would say. Had he detected an Irish accent as well?

Unbelievable. Now he was being haunted by the intrusive ghosts of his late relatives.

* * * *

"I think crushed pecans would really help to keep the breasts tender." Ginny finished putting away the clean kitchenware while Emile sat upon a stool, writing notes for a recipe they were pulling out of thin air. "I have nearly a half-cup left over from last night's dessert."

Rory had just finished restocking the pantry with the newest arrivals while Madam Simone and the others equipped the cold storage and the wine cellar.

Ginny stretched to reach a hook with the handle of a cast-iron pan not a foot from Emile.

"And almonds, I understand, are very good for the consumer's complexion." Emile reached out and cupped Ginny's cheek with the palm of his hand. "Slivered, they would add yet another appealing texture to the stuffing."

She beamed at Emile and he stroked her cheek with his thumb before he released her.

Rory gritted his teeth. The Frenchie shouldn't be touching her in such an intimate manner. But if he uttered a single word of protest it would push Ginny further away from him and make wooing her completely impossible. *Why can't I think of clever things to say to Ginny?* Why was it always Emile at the right place and the right time? Why—

"Monsieur Hughson?"

Torn from his jealous musings, Rory snapped his gaze to Emile's. "Yes?"

"Please take a half-cup of almonds and cut them in to tiny slivers, would you?"

"Slivers?"

"Well, they might not all end up stick-like, but do your best." He turned back to Ginny and they continued chatting.

By the time Rory finished his task, Ginny and Emile were already gathering the pantry items for the rest of the dish. They came together to take one more look at the recipe.

Wedging himself between Ginny and the Frenchie, Rory presented the almonds to Emile.

Seemingly unaffected by the action, Emile praised Rory's efforts. "You did very well. You have a fine hand for the smaller jobs. I noticed this last week when you handled stuffing the game hens so well."

Rory nodded his thanks, but was sure Emile's words held another meaning, such as an insult to his person.

Emile set a hand on both Rory and Ginny's shoulders. "You two combine the dry ingredients in a large bowl. I will fetch the remaining ingredients from cold storage."

The second Emile was out of earshot, Rory lodged his complaint with Ginny. "My hands aren't small. In point of fact, they are quite big." He demonstrated by holding his hands out in front of her and flipping them back and forth. "Imagine him saying that to me."

"Oh, Rory, Emile didn't call your hands small." Ginny poured both cups of nuts into the bowl.

"Well, where I come from, fine means small. One should never refer to another man's...anything as small. Especially not another man. Had he any manners whatsoever, he would know better." Rory passed her the ground rosemary, salt and sage she'd chopped and combined earlier.

"You don't understand him the way I do, Rory." Ginny added the herbs and chose a wooden spoon from a drawer. She handed it to Rory.

"How could I? He doesn't whisk me away to dark corners, whisper in my ear and play with my hair."

To his astonishment, Ginny doubled over with laughter. When she recovered, she asked. "Would you like him to?"

Emile and Madam Simone arrived with their arms full. Ginny sobered quickly and went to help them while Rory blended what was in the bowl.

"Virginia, I had a revelation about our impromptu recipe."

"Do tell," she said taking the platter of poultry breasts layered with ice chips from him and placing it on the counter.

"I thought we could fold our mixture into some *fromage frais*. Then we'll thin the breasts with a meat mallet, spread the herbs, nuts and cheese over the meat and fold them over like pastries before we cook them."

"Mmm. Sounds wonderful."

Rory spoke up. "I'll volunteer to pound the meat."

Emile's brow rose over an inquisitive eye. "Will you, now?" he drawled.

Virginia cleared her throat. "I'll show you how, Rory. We don't want to end up with poultry paste, after all."

"Very well. Madam Simone and I will prepare the roasted potatoes and garlic butter sauce."

After putting on a huge pot of water to boil, Ginny set her and Rory up in a corner away from what Madame Simone dubbed the potato station.

"We'll have to work fast. Poultry is prone to go bad quickly at room temperature." She pulled out a clean cutting board and placed it upon the counter.

"I don't want to talk about chicken, Ginny."

"Good, because it's turkey. And call me Virginia. Hand me two mallets, please." She indicated to the utensils which hung from pegs on the wall.

He did as she asked. "I also don't wish to quibble about names."

She handed him one. "That suits me fine. I'm glad you haven't concerned yourself about Emile and me using each other's first names." She shook the ice chips off a slab of turkey and laid it upon the cutting board.

"Ah, here is a subject I'd like to discuss."

"Now, we are not out to beat the meat into oblivion, only re-shape it." She began tapping the edges of the meat, working her way into the centre and back out again. "Take one and try it, but gently."

"You are changing the subject." He began tapping at the meat.

"The subject at hand is turkey."

"The subject is you and that snake."

"I don't know how to cook snake."

"Ginny!" he ground out and slammed the mallet down onto the turkey.

"Rory!" she emulated his harsh tone. "Don't pound so hard, you'll pulverise the meat."

Rory took hold of both mallets and tossed them onto the counter. "May I see you outside, *Miss* Clark?"

Chapter Fourteen

It wasn't a demand, but Rory certainly didn't give Virginia a choice, as he was now hauling her out of the door by her wrist.

"Is this entirely necessary?" she hissed as they crossed the threshold.

Rory shut the kitchen door none too gently. "It is. I've had just about enough of you and that Frenchie. He's too forward with you and you let him, even encourage it."

"We are friends, Rory. For Heaven's sake, it's not as if he's made formal overtures to me."

"And just what exactly do you mean by formal?"

She blinked at him and the revelation hit home. "You're jealous of Emile. That's it, isn't it?"

He groaned. "Of course not."

"Well, if that's not your point of aggravation, what is? It's not as if he's put me in any compromising situation. My life has not been put in jeopardy while in his presence, not even close. So the only assumption I can make is that you are jealous."

Rory folded his arms across his chest. "If he treated everyone including the servers in the same manner he treats you, I wouldn't have cause to complain. But while he romances you with food and candlelight and treats you like a queen, he has the rest of us cleaning, chopping, peeling and stuffing things."

"That is the way of a culinary hierarchy. You will just have to live with it. Remember, you were the one who insisted on tagging along in the first place." She made to go around him but he stopped her by stepping into her path.

"I believe he thinks to take my place."

"As what, my chaperone?"

"No. As your—"

"Virginia?" Emile's voice came from the kitchen door. "Are you finished with the turkey breasts?"

She whipped around. "Not yet." She strode around Rory. "Let me make one more pass at them, Emile. I'll have them ready for you right away." She turned from Rory without so much as a 'by your leave', but she didn't care. It was her way of reciprocating his rudeness.

Back in the kitchen, she made fast work of the rest of the meat, but wished it was Rory beneath her mallet. *Why is he continually angry with me? I've done nothing untoward*, she grumbled to herself. *Why all the mystery, and why did he have to place blame on Emile? Emile is innocent of any suspicious charges — and besides, he treats me the way a woman should be treated. Why can't Rory treat me that way?*

Glancing around, she noticed that Rory hadn't come back into the kitchen. Fine. Let him steep somewhere else.

She handed Emile the thinned-out breasts and tossed the mallets and cutting board into one of the sinks, then poured the entire pot of boiling water over them.

Virginia stared into the rising steam. What was Rory trying to say? Pity it wasn't a declaration of love. His constant reprimands were far too demeaning to be reflective of such a delicate emotion. She pondered his last half-statement to her, before Emile interrupted them. Rory said he thought Emile wanted to take his place. As what? *The big brother I never had? My best friend?*

She blew out a frustrated breath, disrupting the upward flow of condensation before her. Nothing made sense.

The sound of the oven closing brought Virginia out of her thoughts.

"The potatoes are roasting. What is for dessert, my angel?" Emile had come up behind her and placed his hands upon her shoulders. He worked the tight muscles there as if kneading dough.

Virginia closed her eyes. "Ah, that feels lovely. I don't know. What shall we have with our nutty, cheesy poultry pockets?"

"How about you? You look sweet," he said in a most seductive and teasing manner that sent tingles over her skin.

She laughed aloud and turned to Emile to reply, but the tart retort lodged in her throat. Rory stood behind them with a stack of clean towels. He arched a brow at her, tossed the linens onto the counter, stalked across the room and took the stairs two at a time. Rory, the perpetually angry rattlesnake.

"Was Madame Simone able to obtain that brick of chocolate?" she asked flatly, her mind on Rory's exit.

"She did. I wrapped it in cheese cloth and placed it in cold storage."

"Good. I think I'll make a chocolate soufflé." Ignoring the sour taste Rory had left in her mouth, she squared her shoulders to tackle the task at hand.

* * * *

Rory hadn't spoken a single word to her in almost two weeks. Virginia wasn't sure she was content or dissatisfied with his silence. She'd caught him glaring at her a few times from across the kitchen, but it was usually when Emile stood by as they cooked and laughed together.

Emile and Virginia's Poultry Pockets had been such a success, Monsieur Leroux had requested them for supper no fewer than three times. On each occasion when Emile announced the menu to the staff, Virginia caught Rory's scowl. Perhaps if Rory had participated in the initial creation instead of lurking about with his ever-present frown, the dish wouldn't be referred to as 'Emile and Virginia's Poultry Pockets'.

She refused to carry the guilt on her shoulders. Rory could pout all he wanted.

While Virginia scraped at one of the pre-soaked food-encrusted pots from this evening's meal, Monsieur Antonio, the painter, poked his head into the kitchen.

"Ah, Monsieur, can I get you anything else? More wine, perhaps?" Virginia asked as she wiped soapy hands on her apron.

"No, no. The wonderful meal filled me sufficiently… But I was wondering…"

The kitchen activities slowed around her, likely so that everyone could hear what Monsieur Antonio wished to say. "Yes?" she asked, anticipatory as well.

From behind him, Gaston hastily ushered Antonio into the room. "Come now, Antonio, do not be afraid to ask such a harmless question. Now, out with it."

"Don't be so pushy, *mon ami*. She may not be interested in participating."

"Well, all one can do is ask. Go on then."

Virginia felt Rory come to stand just behind her. The last thing she wanted was for him to put his nose into her business. Determined to make her own decision about whatever it was Gaston and Antonio were going on about, she strode toward them. "Gentlemen, what is it you'd like to ask?"

Antonio drew in a breath then let his query out all at once. "I was wondering if you would sit for me, that is all."

Before Virginia even had a chance to react, Rory stepped up. "No."

"Excuse me, Mr Hughson, but I don't believe you were invited to be part of this conversation." She turned back to the inquisitive men. "Yes, I would be happy to."

"No, she wouldn't," Rory retorted.

"I do beg your pardon, *Monsieurs*." She smiled at them and spun on Rory. "You are dismissed for the evening, sir."

Rory completely ignored her and spoke to them over her head. "It isn't proper for a young woman to be alone in a room with a man who is, for lack of a better term, a stranger. I believe you have your answer, gentlemen."

Virginia struggled to keep her protest to a modest sound level. "We've been here for weeks. I know Monsieur as well as I know…" Virginia's voice trailed off. She almost inserted Rory's name into that scenario, which would have opened an entire barrel of rotten apples she'd never hear the end of.

Like a knight in service of his damsel, Emile entered into the conversation. "Perhaps, Monsieurs, if Rory was asked to pose with Virginia, it would not seem so scandalous to him."

Every questioning gaze in the room landed on Rory. Had he not been washing dishes in a hot kitchen, Virginia would have sworn his face reddened. One would think he'd have learnt by now not to stick his nose in where it didn't belong. Every time he did, he ended up doing something he wasn't ready to commit to. She smirked. He'd never agree to sitting for a painting, not in a hundred years.

"Fine. When do we start?"

Had Virginia's jaw not been properly hinged to her skull, it would have plunged to the terracotta floor. She choked. "You can't mean—"

"I do." For a brief moment his gaze scanned her from head to toe. Then he turned to Gaston and Antonio. "Those are my terms, gentlemen."

Antonio tilted his head and folded his arms across his chest in contemplation. Then he stroked a hand down his bushy moustache. "This could work well."

Gaston clapped his hands together and rubbed away a feigned chill. "Superb. When do you want them, Antonio?"

Antonio solicited Emile for his opinion with an upturned hand.

"I would be willing to give them up, say, tomorrow between breakfast and luncheon."

"Perfect!" Antonio grinned. "Both of you meet me in the east drawing room after breakfast."

"Will this be a formal portrait or should we come as we are?" Rory asked.

Virginia still had not found her voice.

"I think, perhaps…" Antonio squinted at his models. "Bring two of your best waistcoats, and bring your cleanest shirt and cravat. I will have a gown for Mademoiselle Clark."

With that, Antonio and Gaston left the kitchen. In their wake stood a smug-faced Rory, a grinning Emile and Virginia, who could feel angry heat rising from the top of her head like steam from a well-ventilated pie.

Chapter Fifteen

Rory caught up with Ginny as she hurried through the hallway on her way to the east drawing room. "Where do you think you are going?" he asked, grasping his wardrobe as if it were a lifeline.

She hesitated but only for a moment. "Where do you think?"

"I think you were rushing into that room to try and talk this artist out of allowing me to participate."

"Ha!" Her voice cracked. "Whatever gave you that idea?"

"Because, Miss Clark, whether you approve of the notion or no, I know you, and I know what you would do, given the chance. You'd try and oust me from the room as quick as I could snap my fingers."

"Don't be ridiculous."

"Then why are you practically running?"

She shortened her footsteps, hoping he wouldn't notice when she peeked up at him to see if he had. His gaze briefly rolled across the frescoed ceiling of the hall.

Ignoring his reaction, she searched for an answer. "I...I wanted to see what sort of gown I would be sitting in."

"You don't lie very well, you know that?"

"Oh, stop your needling. Don't you dare make a scene in front of Monsieur —"

"Do not worry about me. I can hide my thoughts well."

Virginia reached for the doorknob to the sitting room and grasped it tightly. "That, sir, is not a virtue, but a flaw." She tossed the door open before he could protest.

Antonio stood at one end of the room. His artist tools scattered about him, the area he would use as his backdrop was immaculate. Furniture and cushions had been pushed to the other side of the room to accommodate the scene.

"Ah, welcome." He walked towards them and studied both of their faces. "No need to be nervous, you two. I promise to make this as painless as possible."

"Nervous?" Ginny chuckled woodenly. "We're not nervous."

"I would never go against the word of a lady, but you and Monsieur Hughson are scowling."

Ginny's gaze met Rory's, but only for a moment.

"Come. Let me show you my thoughts and then perhaps you can relax a little, eh?" He brought them to a stunning red velvet fainting couch beneath an east-facing window. Covering the window was a solid, walnut privacy screen and sheer, white curtains were pulled forward to hug each end of the couch. They stood before the scene and Rory heard Ginny give a little sigh of delight at the sight. It was a familiar sound, a sound he'd drawn from her a time or two. His groin gave a twitch at the thought.

"If Mademoiselle would step behind the brocade privacy screen, there you will find your costume."

Ginny did as he bid.

Antonio turned to Rory. "Now, what have you brought me?"

Rory held up the only two acceptable-in-front-of-company waistcoats he'd brought. "I have this cardinal and gold, and this black."

"Hm. The black has a unique texture to it. Let me see it on you."

While Rory slipped on the waistcoat, Ginny emerged from behind the screen.

"I'm afraid this gown is a bit big, Monsieur. I believe it was meant to be worn off the shoulders, but it doesn't quite meet either of them." She held the azure blue silk bodice in place with both hands. The fabric of the dress would have gaped were she not pressing it against her chest.

Rory almost groaned at the sight of Ginny's bare, creamy-white shoulders and elegant neck. It had been so long since he'd enjoyed the view.

"Come and sit, Mademoiselle. We can give the illusion that it fits."

The last button was in place and Rory couldn't help but gaze at Ginny's smooth skin as he watched her recline against an emerald and silver tasselled pillow.

Antonio chuckled. "Monsieur, you have mismatched your buttons with the corresponding holes."

Rory looked down. He was off by two buttonholes and it made the waistcoat appear lopsided. He unbuttoned the vest as fast as his fingers could fly.

"Wait one moment." Antonio held up a hand. "Take it off again."

He shrugged out of the waistcoat, tossed it onto the floor and waited for the painter to tell him what to do next.

"Remove your cravat." Antonio stepped over to Ginny and began arranging her and the gown around her. Rory's cravat tie fell to the ground next to his waistcoat. "Now, come sit next to her."

Rory took his place, not knowing if he would survive the next couple of hours this close to the naked shoulders of the love of his life.

"You, Mademoiselle, have the easy part. All you have to do is lean back against the pillow and relax."

Antonio placed one of Ginny's legs across Rory's thighs. The intimacy brought back vibrant, delicious memories to Rory. He would commission a hundred paintings from Antonio to know Ginny's thoughts.

"Monsieur, I want you to face Mademoiselle Clark. Good. Now lean towards her and rest your forearm on the back of the couch. Yes. Perfect."

His face hovered near hers. He could feel her trembling from where he gazed down at her and it melted his insides like butter in a hot iron pan. Regardless of the fact that he hadn't seen her wild side since his youth, he knew exactly what lay beneath that prim façade she kept so perfectly in place.

Everything that made up her personality, coupled with her beauty, made her so damn alluring to him. Rory was glad his rapidly stiffening cock was buried beneath her skirts, well out of view of the company in the room.

For a moment or two, the painter remained silent. Rory felt his scrutiny from across the room and was tempted to glance at Antonio. It wasn't long until the intimate dance between pencil and sketch tablet whispered in the strained atmosphere.

"Tell me, how did you two meet?" Antonio asked, no doubt attempting to relax them.

A soft sigh escaped Ginny and she shut her eyes, as if refusing to answer.

It was up to him now to deflect rumours that might arise from her silence. Rory spoke without looking away from Ginny. "We were introduced by my brother's wife."

At once her eyes popped open. A pleased grin settled upon her lips. Rory was certain she felt gratitude for his discreet answer.

"You seem to know each other very well," Antonio commented. "How long have you been acquainted?"

"Nearly all of our lives," he said aloud, then whispered so that only Ginny could hear, "I hope his questions end here. I'd hate to have to go into detail about our familiarity."

Rory watched the colour in Ginny's cheeks rise to a boil. Her smile faded, but still revealed nothing of what she was thinking.

"Yes, that's perfect!" Antonio cried out. "Whatever you said to her, don't stop. She has a delicious blush staining her cheeks, and you, Monsieur, are wearing a most devastating rogue's grin. I wish to capture you exactly this way."

"Don't you dare," Ginny whispered to Rory and averted her gaze.

Rory couldn't help but chuckle. "We must do as the doctor orders, my dear."

Her eyes flashed back to his, her eyelids narrowed in anger. "He's not a doctor, Rory," she fairly growled.

"Mon Dieu." Antonio's quiet laughter floated over to them. "My friends, the mood you've created is an artist's utopia. The two of you look as if you are going to either kill each other or make love right there on the couch."

"Ginny," Rory whispered, pushing aside the painter's enticing suggestion. He'd waited for the perfect opportunity to discuss his affections for her, but she seemed to avoid it at every turn. How ironic that his captive audience had come so willingly today. "Tell me what you remember about the carriage ride to Tucson."

"I won't do this with you."

Little did she know, her warning fell onto deaf ears.

"Then I will recount the tale for you." He watched her mouth draw into a tight line, but disregarded the action. "I remember how surprised I was when you emerged from beneath the pile of coats on the bench opposite me, mere moments after the journey began."

"Rory—"

"The shy look in your eyes in direct contrast to your tempting tongue as it moistened your full lips."

"I don't remember licking my lips. You exaggerate."

The scent of the oil paints reached him, but he continued. "I'm telling my side of the story. Now hush."

"No. I won't listen to this."

"So you'll break our pose and frustrate Antonio, all because you refuse to contribute to our conversation?"

"I wouldn't be so disagreeable to Antonio."

"Then—"

"However, I do refuse to listen!" she hissed.

No matter the consequences, there was no way he would stop now. Rory glanced down. The curve of her breasts above the ill-fitting bodice rose and fell with her short, rapid breaths. He stifled a growl and after following the contours of her exposed décolletage, his gaze languidly returned to hers.

"I wondered what you were doing there, and when I asked you, you just smiled." Ginny didn't move. "Then you moved over to my side and sat next to me, the skirt of that innocent little ivory and brown calico dress draped over my leg, you were so close."

"Truly, it is unnecessary to remind me of my lapse in—"

"I couldn't even breathe when you leaned towards me."

"Rory," Ginny pleaded.

"Then you asked me to kiss you. What was I to say to the enchantress before me?"

"Enchantress? Hardly," Ginny murmured as if she could stem the tide of his account.

"Even so, if you asked for the world on a platter I wouldn't have denied you."

The air heated between them like an oven, but he continued. "You pressed your body to mine. Do you remember the first place I kissed you?"

"Yes," she breathed. "My sh...shoulder."

"To be precise, it was the spot just between your shoulder and neck. It was one of the sweetest, softest places my lips had ever been."

Rory heard the slight catch in her breath and continued.

"I kissed every inch of your exposed neck twice over."

Ginny swallowed hard.

"Do you remember what happened next?"

The tiniest whimper escaped from the back of her throat.

"I whispered something in your ear."

"Liar. You did not."

He felt his grin blossom to a full-blown smile. "So, you do remember."

Ginny pressed her lips together.

"I wanted to. I wanted to tell you how much I liked kissing you."

"Stop. Now."

"That's not what you said in the cab of that bouncy ride. In fact, you seemed to like my kisses. *Very* much."

"Oh, Rory, for God's sake." Her harsh whisper pleaded with him.

"You were the first girl I'd been that close to, the first girl I ever wanted to kiss..."

"Rory—"

"Do you remember how we fumbled through it, learning how to kiss together?"

She closed her eyes and didn't breathe for a moment or two.

Good God, Ace had been right. Rory wanted the steamy hoyden that dwelt beneath the skin of the woman before him, not the daughters and granddaughters of his aunt Iris's friends. There was no point in denying himself any further. He leaned towards her and kissed her beautiful mouth.

Ginny gasped and pressed her hand to his chest. "Please..." she said against his lips.

He pulled back, if only a few inches.

Apparently, the action pleased Antonio. "Superb. Hold the pose, just like that."

Chapter Sixteen

His heart beat beneath her hand fast and powerful. Her thumb and forefinger rested inside the open V of his shirt. Rory's skin felt like hot satin. Had she not already been reclined on a fainting couch, she would have swooned. How many times had she repeated their innocent yet amorous kisses in her mind? She inhaled his scent for the umpteenth time since they'd sat down together. Her proper façade teetered on shaky ground.

"Then you began running your tongue along my ear."

"Shall you cause me to recount all of my misbehaviour, and relive the guilt?"

"You made me squirm, my mind was going in all directions at once."

"That's enough, Rory. Some things shouldn't be said aloud." This was neither the time nor the place for such dangerous games. Didn't he realise that?

He ignored her, just as he had since he'd began his daring recollection. She needed to hear it, he was sure...and he needed to inspire her heart, to bring the woman he'd once known back into his life, back into his arms. "I could have died right there when you wrapped your arms around my neck and pulled me closer."

She drew in a shuddering breath. The room simply shimmered with heat, her eyesight blurring to everything but his piercing blue eyes.

"Looking back, I would have given anything to stay the entire night with you in that carriage." His whispered words were so soft she felt them blow across her face.

Virginia couldn't draw enough cool air into her fevered body and stop the room from spinning.

"My Ginny. I will never forget how you made me feel. You were...like a fantasy. Our passion was so intense, so real. And it can be again."

All at once, Antonio broke Rory's spell from across the room. "You are welcome to take a break now. I am going to fetch something cool for us to drink."

Virginia untangled herself from Rory and perched on the edge of the couch. She grasped the gown to her chest. "I'll come with you."

"Are you certain, Mademoiselle? I feel I've interrupted a conversation between you and —"

"No, no. Besides, I...I need some air." She rose and practically ran from the room, not looking back at the seductive man still on the couch.

All too soon she and Antonio were headed back to the drawing room from the kitchen. Antonio pushed the tea cart topped with iced lemonade, courtesy of Emile. Virginia's steps were slow as if each of her feet weighed as much as immensely large cheese wheels. She held her arms folded over her chest to help keep the bodice from gaping open.

Antonio cleared his throat. "You make a lovely art model, Mademoiselle."

"Please, Monsieur. There is no need to flatter me."

"I cannot help but tell the truth," he said casually from behind the cart.

Just outside the drawing room door, Virginia came to a halt and turned to the painter, stopping him in his tracks. "I appreciate the chance to model, but I want you to know, Monsieur, I do not plan on sitting for you beyond this single project."

"Were you uncomfortable? Was it the dress? Perhaps I can—"

"No, no. It was nothing to do with you."

"Was it your lover, then?"

Virginia nearly choked. "We...we are not lovers, Monsieur."

"Mademoiselle, I am a man. I can tell when another man is in love. It shows in the eyes. Can you not see it when he looks at you?"

She couldn't help but release a strangled laugh. "If Monsieur Hughson was in love with me, wouldn't he have declared it by now?"

"Perhaps, if he were a Frenchman."

His odd comment took her aback. "What on earth does that mean?"

"Monsieur Hughson may be the shy type." He shrugged.

Rory, shy? That would be the day. "I assure you, Monsieur Hughson is anything but shy."

Virginia and Antonio turned as the door to the drawing room opened.

"I thought I heard voices out here." Rory smiled amicably.

Without a word, Virginia strode past him to the fainting couch while Antonio wheeled the tea cart inside.

Rory and Antonio sipped Emile's lemonade over polite conversation while Virginia fidgeted with her gown.

Finally, the moment she was dreading, the moment when Rory came to hover over her, arrived. Antonio arranged them as they had been before the break, then stepped behind his easel once again.

"You didn't have any lemonade." Rory commented.

"Emile had me taste it in the kitchen. I drank some then."

"Mmm," came Rory's enigmatic reply.

"Where is that blush, Mademoiselle? I need it back," Antonio half-teased from across the room.

"Can I help with that?" Rory inquired of Antonio.

"*S'il vous plait.*"

Rory grinned down at her. "Now, where were we?"

"Nowhere," she murmured defiantly.

"Strange, I remember. Our interrupted conversation left us in the carriage on the way to Tucson."

"Ah, that's the blush. You are good, Monsieur Hughson." Virginia could hear the grin in Antonio's voice. She knew he was trying to prove what he had said to her in the hallway about Rory being in love with her.

Ha. Lust perhaps, but it couldn't possibly be love.

"I couldn't stop kissing you, couldn't stop saying your name."

"Perhaps you need more practice stopping. You can start stopping right now."

Rory chuckled. "I'd rather have more practice kissing you."

She refused to laugh, so she glanced down at his smiling mouth instead. She couldn't have possibly known the temptation that awaited her there. God, how she wanted to give in to his suggestion.

"Did I leave anything out?"

Virginia swallowed. "Yes, when the door opened at our destination and Beatrice's eyes flashed lightning at me, and your father and brother looked as if they wanted to beat you all the way back to Virginia."

"No," he whispered, his eyes shining with humour. "I mean before that, when we had been so exhausted from being in each other's arms…and had to open the window to relieve us of the sultry air in the cab. We were so drowsy afterwards, you and I."

She wanted him so badly, his lips, his body. She nearly let the admission slip out, however, the room spun and tilted crazily. As providence would have it, the words stalled in her throat. "You've made your point."

He continued to ignore her. "Do you remember the sweet things you whispered to me… Your soft voice nearly made me go insane. We could have done some very real damage that day, and I'm sure I wouldn't have minded in the least."

His wicked, whispered words buzzed in her ears, eliciting waves of goose bumps over her skin. "No, we shouldn't be talking about this," she breathed and averted her gaze from his face to stare at the ceiling beyond his head. His verbal recollection was more than she could bear, and she almost told him so. But she was in enough trouble as it was.

Rory nuzzled her cheek with his nose, then pulled away to look into her eyes once again. "God, your innocence, your scent, your lips… I thought I would expire from the ecstasy of it."

He'd gone as far as he could. Her lust boiled to the surface of her skin, alive, tangible. Rory Hughson had splintered her determination to uphold propriety, the very same propriety his own brother's wife had instilled in her. And damn it, he'd already brought her to the brink of a confession. She dared not even squirm in her seat. The slightest movement would surely give her away.

"I want to make love to you. Let me, Ginny. Please?"

Virginia's mouth went dry. Yes, she wanted him, so intensely she shook inside.

The door to the drawing room closed. Their attention was drawn to the noise.

Antonio had left them alone in the room.

She gasped.

He pressed his body to hers, pinning her to the couch. "I'll give him this, he's a smart man."

At once, his lips met hers and, though her head screamed that she should not participate, she kissed him back, knowing exactly where it would lead. She felt the hem of the dress she wore slide up her thigh. She broke out of the kiss. "No, Rory. Not here."

"Here is as good a place as any." He panted the words. "And certainly better than kissing in a cramped carriage."

"But Antonio...or someone is sure to come in."

"Then I shall lock out the world." Rory jumped up and in four strides he made it to the door. He twisted the brass key, pulled it from the lock and dropped it onto a small table next to the door.

Virginia took advantage of the opportunity and attempted to cool her ardour. She rose to see what Antonio had painted. However, it appeared he had taken his work with him when he left the room. To the right of the empty easel a handful of paint brushes soaked in a jar of strong-smelling fluid. To the left sat Antonio's still-wet palette adorned with all the colours of the scene she'd just stepped from. A note attached with a clothes pin to the frame of the easel read, "Finished for the day." Virginia murmured the message aloud.

Rory's hands snaked around her waist from behind. "You can't deny now that we won't be interrupted."

Her heart pounded in her ears. Panic that she might give in welled in her stomach. She just *had* to remain immune to his advances if she were going to survive the rest of the summer by his side! "We have to get back to the kitchen."

"No. They aren't expecting us for at least an hour. Look at me, Ginny." He spun her around.

Her gaze travelled up his chest to the smooth skin of his jaw to his riveting azure eyes.

Rory pulled her against his body. "I've waited forever to have you again," he murmured.

And damn it if he wasn't kissing her once more, making her lose her wits.

Chapter Seventeen

The last remaining shreds of Virginia's long-suffering, prim and proper pretence fell away and she surrendered to the one man who had, since she could remember, occupied her baser thoughts, the handsome Rory Hughson.

Since the moment they'd sat down on that couch he'd drawn her in, like the pull of the tides to the moon. Bliss replaced the guilt she'd felt earlier. The giddiness of her youth crept in. The grand romance she shared with Rory, however brief, blazed to life in her veins.

With Rory's assistance, the borrowed dress slipped effortlessly over her hips to the floor. Her drawers followed. Virginia stood in her corset and stockings and pressed her body to his. She trembled in anticipation of what they were about to do.

He gently raised her hand to his lips then guided her to the pillows strewn about before the fireless hearth and lowered her to the Persian rug. On their knees, he took her in his arms once again and kissed her, at the same time untying the bow at the top of her corset.

She broke out of the kiss and inhaled a shuddering breath, stretching the laces across her back. Once the hooks and eyes in front gave way, he gathered the trapping and tossed it aside. She reclined, and the cool satin of a pillow against her heated skin made her breath catch. The fluffy pillow situated at her lower back caused her belly to arch toward him.

Rory's hands skimmed over her body. "Pity we can't take all night. Had we that luxury, I'd take you on a spiritual journey to the heavens."

"You're not taking me anywhere until your clothes are on the floor next to mine." She grinned.

"Ah, a greedy little hoyden, eh?"

Virginia giggled at his brazen statement. While he shed his shirt and pants, Virginia turned over onto her belly. It felt wonderful to unchain her manners and let her inhibitions run amok. Although another indiscretion, however brief, could lead to more complications for her…

She felt him stretch out next to her. "Where'd you go?"

"I'm here." She rolled onto her side, her back to his front. "I was just thinking."

"Hm." The tips of his fingers began drawing lazy circles across her back. The sensation sent waves of goose bumps cascading over the edge of her ribs, straight to her nipples. "How can I dissuade you from doing so?"

"I can't stop thinking, Rory. We are adults now. There are many things to consider." His fingernails scratched tickling lines up and down her back. Virginia felt herself sinking in to a luxurious, seductive sensation she'd never felt before. Her nipples practically buzzed with awareness.

"That's just it. We are adults. Fear of retribution has no place between us."

Then he placed a kiss in the centre of her back and followed her spine up to her neck, dragging his lips along her flesh. She could discern when he would exhale and inhale. His tongue darted out every so often to tease her.

"Besides, I can think of no better way to spend an hour." His kisses trailed back down to her lower back and his fingers started their tickling trails once again.

Virginia shivered, her body absorbing every tingly touch. When she could take no more of his fingertips skimming across her skin, she moaned and lay on her back.

Rory gazed at her breasts and ran the back of his hand down between them. A tiny squeak escaped her throat.

"You're so beautiful," he said and bent his head to lick at the puckered tips.

He kissed and suckled and soon she was nearly out of her mind with need. She laced her fingers through his hair, her arms bringing her breasts close together.

"Ginny," he whispered against her skin.

"Kiss me, Rory."

His mouth trailed kisses all the way up to her lips. She slid her hands to his hard shoulders.

Rolling her to the side, he pressed lips to her neck. Virginia reached down and took hold of his cock. She heard his breath catch and felt him pulse in her hand. His hard extremity felt hot to the touch. She cradled him, her fingers wrapped nearly all the way around its thickness.

In a flash, Rory draped her top leg over his hip. She gasped when his fingers found her feminine centre. He inhaled and murmured something she couldn't fully discern. Had he uttered the word 'love'? She tried to recall what he'd said when he slipped from her palm and scooted down her body.

When Rory kissed her mound and lower, she moaned. "Oh, yes." She'd wanted this for what seemed like an eternity. "Do it like that." His wiggly tongue snaked up down and around her clitoris and she drew in great gulps of air. Rory held her there with the pressure of his mouth, suckling, licking, worshiping her. The second he latched on she came, her entire body pulsating with sensation.

Ever so slowly, he released her as her spasms eased to mere tremors. Her heart thundered in her ears, her lungs expanding and contracting with every laboured breath.

"I must have you. Now." Rory moved between her legs, guiding himself to the sensitised juncture of her thighs.

"Yes," she hissed, not wanting to wait a second longer. She raised her leg and wrapped it around his waist.

He entered her in one swift movement and Virginia went off again, this time from inside. She'd never felt ecstasy like this, and it was all due to Rory's lovemaking. He rocked into her, her name rolling off his tongue in between gasps. Her body opened to his thick penis, her core closing around him as if trying to hold him inside.

His breathing matched his body's motion and she let herself sink into the sensation. "You are so strong, I love the way you dominate me."

Rory merely growled, which she found absolutely primitive.

At once he pressed his chest to hers, his hips still working his cock in and out. "I didn't know you could feel this amazing. God, Ginny. I don't want it to end."

Virginia's mouth grazed his shoulder, then his neck. He turned his head to the side and she took his earlobe between her lips. She sucked at it, the same way he did between her legs. He must have liked it, for he drove into her without mercy.

Her insides convulsed and she voiced her approval. He turned his head towards her and buried his face between her neck and shoulder, letting loose a string of passionate utterances. Somehow she detected the word 'fuck' in amongst his murmurings. It brought back the feelings she had in that carriage. Her mind spun with how naughty she was being right now, but her inhibitions need not be reined in. She wanted this, wanted to keep him as close as humanly possible for as long as she could.

"Rory," she panted. "Are you fucking me?"

His head came up but his body kept moving. "I am."

"I like it when you fuck me."

"You do...?"

"Yes. Don't stop. Fuck me... Fuck me. Make me come."

"Oh, God, Ginny—"

She'd brazenly turned up his fires to broil and he pounded into her with such force it stole her breath away. Another intense wave of orgasms hit her. She cried out, and Rory followed her to the sky.

* * * *

It wasn't long until Virginia rose to gather her clothes. What the hell had she just done? Reality hit like an axe blow to a chicken neck. The thought nagged at her that she'd spent too much time away from her job today. In addition to the mounting guilt, she'd now have to try and quell her desire to repeat the tryst with Rory lest she suffer the loss of her position in the kitchen. Rory was everything she'd dreamt of, but her work must come first if she wanted to make a name for herself. A sideways glance to the spot she'd just vacated told her Rory had risen to gather his clothes as well.

They dressed in silence. She laid the borrowed dress across the fainting couch and took one last lingering look at the scene she'd sat for. Virginia was positive she'd lose her head again if Antonio wanted them to sit for another session. She prayed that what he'd achieved today would be enough to satisfy him.

Virginia was sure Antonio knew what they had done, after all, it was he himself who'd practically thrown her and Rory together.

How was it that every craving, every carnal thought she'd learnt to stomp down for the last few years just bubbled to the surface with hardly any effort whatsoever? She was an adult, for Heavens' sakes. And there was work to be done. Work that was important to her.

"Penny for your thoughts?"

She shrugged a shoulder, finding it unnecessary to voice what was on her mind. "I need to get back to the kitchen." Virginia walked over to the door and picked up the key from the table.

"How about if later tonight, we—"

"Rory, this ends here. We've indulged the needs of the flesh and we mustn't do it again." She slipped the key into the lock.

He stepped toward her. "But I—"

"Please understand, Rory. I cannot be distracted. I have a job to do."

Rory blew out a breath. "Fine. But when we return to the States—"

"You will be quite bored with me by then, I'm sure." She turned the key, opened the door and quit the room, unable to think beyond dessert tonight, let alone the end of summer.

On the way back to the kitchen, she admitted to herself that her ludicrous statement had been issued because she was angrier with herself than with Rory. Beatrice would be terribly disappointed in her, were she to find out that Virginia had backslid from the lady she'd helped her become. She should stay far away from Rory and his seductive ways, and not think of him at all. Put him completely out of her mind. Perhaps she'd banish him to cold storage. Hell, she should banish herself to cold storage.

Virginia almost laughed aloud at herself. The only reason it was easy to declare what she should and shouldn't do was because she'd just been sexually satisfied. Her body felt content, thoroughly made love to, utterly relaxed. In fact, she could lie down and take a nap if she didn't have to get back to her duties. But what would happen in a week, a day or even that night when she found herself with that insatiable urge for more of the heart-stopping orgasms Rory could give her?

Emile looked up from tasting Madame Simone's soup when Virginia entered. He put his spoon down and waved her over. "How was it?"

Virginia thought she'd seen the barest of smirks on his handsome face and nearly choked. "I...I beg your pardon?"

He took her by the hand and led her to the pantry, shutting the door behind them. "Your skin is dusted with a raging blush, my dear, and your eyes reflect a certain fire. Tell me, what has tantalised you so?" he asked, and drew her fingers to his lips.

"Emile, I can't possibly endure your flirting right now. I must get back to work."

"But you look so delicious. Come. You know you can talk to me about anything."

"Look, you rogue," she teased. "I know you'd take my most intimate secret to your heart and never tell anyone."

"You have my word on that."

"Emile." She relaxed against him. "I need you more as a friend right now than anything else."

"I can be whomever you desire, *ma chérie*."

"Yes, you've been proving your diversity with the entire kitchen staff, save for Rory, Madame Simone and I."

"Who told you Madame Simone turned me down?" he demanded with a mock pout.

Virginia laughed. "I don't believe you. You are such a...a..."

"Cad? Ruffian?"

"I was thinking more along the lines of a Romeo, as in Romeo Montague."

"I've been told I fill out tights rather well."

The door to the panty flew open and Virginia pushed away from Emile. Rory stood there, his facial expressions ran the gamut of dark emotions before he spoke. "What is going on in here?"

"Ah, Monsieur. Do join us. We were discussing Shakespearean characters."

Rory glared at Emile. "If you don't wish to personally revisit a Shakespearean tragedy, then you'll remove yourself from this room right now."

"Rory, that's enough." Virginia's voice conveyed the shock she felt at the verbal violence he displayed.

"It's all right, Virginia. I understand. He has every right to be protective." Emile bowed a nod to Rory and took his leave.

Two steps brought Virginia mere inches away from Rory. "For the first time since Emile and I started working together, I must disagree with him. You have no rights whatsoever when it comes to my person, including with whom I choose to speak or where I choose to speak with them." Disallowing Rory to utter a single syllable, she stormed out of the pantry and headed straight for Emile.

"May I have a word with you, Emile, outside?" she said loudly, hoping Rory heard the invitation.

"Of course," Emile answered.

Rory could do naught but stare after Ginny. In front of everyone, she'd deliberately taken Emile by the hand and headed out of doors with him. *What is she playing at? Does she not know how scandalous this sort of thing looks?*

He stopped himself from mentally chastising her. What had he just done with her in the formal drawing room? He'd seduced her right under Antonio's nose, then took full advantage of her lush body while she had been in the vulnerable state he'd lured her into.

However, from the beginning, Rory had harboured no devious intent toward her. He couldn't, with a clear conscience, say that about Emile.

He strode over to the window to try and figure out what was transpiring. Pity he couldn't hear what they were saying.

Chapter Eighteen

"If you feel so strongly, why don't you tell him he is out of line?"

"I have been telling him for weeks now that I'm an adult and should be treated like one."

Emile's gaze wandered to somewhere off in the distance. "My guess is you will not like hearing this, but...you are a delicate flower, *ma chérie*." He looked her in the eye. "It is ingrained in men to protect women, even more so when they deeply care for the one in question."

Virginia deflated. "You have such a way with words, Emile. When you put it that way, his behaviour sounds so innocent."

"Ah, *ma petite*," he murmured as if he was comforting a little girl. He drew her into his arms for a sympathetic embrace.

She let him hold her for a few moments, then pulled away. "And I feel so immature for presenting you with all this childish nonsense."

Emile tutted. "We are friends as well as colleagues. If I am unable to distinguish between the two and

147

know when to switch hats, then I'm not a very good friend, am I?"

"I don't deserve you as either."

He took her hand and gave it a squeeze. "We'll have none of that. You are more deserving than you know." Then he clucked her chin like one would a child. "Now I want you to go on upstairs and rest. In an hour or so, come back down and you can teach me to make those American biscuits I've heard about."

Gaining permission from her superior to take some time to herself couldn't have put her more at ease. She smiled. Releasing his hand, Virginia turned and headed for her room.

Not two minutes after she'd collapsed onto her bed, a knock sounded on her door.

"Who is it?" she called from her face-down position.

"It's Rory."

"What do you want?"

"I want to speak to you."

Virginia smothered a growl. She'd been given a momentary reprieve from her mental turmoil, and a conversation with Rory was not on the menu. Heaving a great sigh she called out, "Come in, then."

He entered and stood at the foot of her bed, fists on his hips. "You are having an affair with him, aren't you?"

"What?" she shrieked and sat bolt upright. "With Emile?"

"Of course with Emile. Who else?"

Her anger boiled over. "Who else, indeed. I've had quite enough of you and your—"

"So, you don't deny it?"

Shaking, Virginia closed her eyes for a moment. "I'm only going to say this once, and if you do not heed my wishes I promise you, I'm going to start throwing things. Get. Out!"

Rory stood there, bold as a well-aged port wine.

She jumped from the bed and reached for her hairbrush. She watched over her shoulder as he strode out of the door, mumbling something about finishing their conversation at a later time.

Virginia released a breath and fell back onto the bed. "How can a man be so terribly blind?"

* * * *

"No."

"Yes. They made love in the east drawing room earlier today."

"How would you know?"

"Let me just say that as they posed for me, I knew I was correct. They are in love."

"So you didn't actually see them doing it."

"Of course not," he scolded, sounding indignant. "Besides I heard the door lock as I stood outside the room."

"For how long did you linger? Did you hear anything else?"

"Come now, Tristan. Are you really that naïve?"

"Well, did you?"

Antonio shrugged. "I heard someone else coming down the corridor and I took my leave."

"This proves nothing."

"Deny it all you want. They are in love and there is nothing you can do about it."

Tristan sighed. "All right, all right. I am man enough to admit defeat."

Antonio clapped him on the back. "You are not defeated. She loved him way before she met you."

Genella deGrey

"Thank you. But that does nothing for my broken heart."

"Broken heart, my ass."

They chuckled together.

"As much as I hate to admit it, it seems that when you pay for sex, your heart is less likely to get involved."

"Have you a fist full of francs?"

"And a pocket full of cock."

Tristan received a blow to the ribs from his friend Antonio.

* * * *

That evening during clean-up, Emile gathered the kitchen staff. "Apparently, a little bird has gone around whispering into certain ears that I'm a decent chef."

Virginia and the others tittered and heckled that the anonymous assumption was correct and quite understated. Rory was in the room somewhere, but she'd managed to ignore his exact whereabouts.

"So it is with regret that I inform you that I've been offered a permanent position at a restaurant in Paris. However…" He paused and held up his hands at the voiced protests. "I would like to extend the invitation to each and every one on this staff to join me there — after you have finished up your duties here at the Leroux château, of course."

A ripple of excitement went through the staff and Virginia felt more than saw Rory come to stand next to her.

Emile went on to tell them about the restaurant, when Rory whispered to her, "So, can we assume you will be going with him?"

150

"I haven't decided," she retorted under her breath without looking at him, knowing full well she wasn't interested in signing up for Emile's venture. Earlier when she and Emile were elbow-deep in biscuit dough, he'd told her his news.

"And why, may I ask, would you presume such a thing?"

"Because of your...*relationship* with him."

Virginia turned to face him. Taking his arm, she practically dragged him to the back of the kitchen away from the others. "You still think I'm having an affair with Emile, don't you? Even after, not hours ago, you and I fornicated in the drawing room?"

"And why not? He's slept with practically every other girl in the kitchen."

For the second time that day, she wanted to knock some sense into him using the closest substantial object. A pity the cast-iron fry pans were across the room. She balled up her fists. "Rory Hughson," she hissed. "You are a horrifying rat."

He laughed woodenly. "What else am I to think? Ever since he arrived, he's been after you."

"Your insinuation that I've reciprocated his sentiments is insulting. Emile and I are only friends."

The gathering at the far end of the kitchen broke into applause then disbursed to finish the evening's chores. Emile headed straight for Virginia and Rory.

"Well, my secret is out," he said affably.

"I'm so very happy for you." Virginia put on her best phony smile. Rory had taken what little joy she'd garnered that afternoon and tossed it out with the dirty dishwater.

"I was wondering if perhaps you would do the market run tomorrow, you and Rory."

"Of course, Emile." Determination to succeed assisted her in setting her melancholy aside. "You filled in for me today, I'd be glad to return the favour."

"Fine," Rory agreed flatly.

"*Merci.* I shall have Madame Simone deliver the list to you. And do not worry about breakfast, I'll have her whip something up for that as well."

All three of them turned to the door to the hallway when Antonio hailed Virginia from across the kitchen. "Ah, there you are." The painter sauntered over to them. "I wanted you to know that the painting is a success, Mademoiselle. It has already been purchased. Much to my happiness, everyone wants one for their very own."

Emile excused himself and Virginia turned to Antonio. "I am indeed flattered, however I wish to be remembered as a chef, not an art model."

Antonio pouted beneath his moustache. "Are you sure you don't want to sit for just one more session?"

"Monsieur, if you want to sketch me, come to the kitchen. That is where I will be. If you will excuse me." Dismissing Antonio, she turned and headed for the sink to discuss the market run with Madame Simone.

Rory, she noticed, had scooped up a drying rag and started on the pots.

It wasn't long before Emile issued the breakfast order to Madame Simone, then went upstairs to retire for the evening.

Rory and Virginia were the last of the staff in the kitchen. Virginia feared another altercation was eminent when Monsieur Hector Guimard, the architect, entered.

"Mademoiselle Clark." He smiled as he approached her, in spite of his timidity. "I hope you don't mind the intrusion, but while Antonio stares at a slow-moving chess match between Gaston and Tristan, I was wondering if you would do me the honour of a tour of this wondrous kitchen. I've seen all the other common rooms but this one."

How could she turn down this nice man, who at every turn had praised her creations, validating her very existence along with the other of Gaston's guests? She drew a breath to acquiesce, when Rory stepped up.

"Allow me to tag along, Monsieur. I, too, have a fondness for this lovely house."

Virginia stood there while Hector accepted Rory's line of lies, wishing for just one bolt of lightning from Heaven.

Chapter Nineteen

In no time she had shown Hector the finer points of the kitchen. Rory had remained blessedly silent the entire time, which suited her well enough. All three of them now stood in the reorganised pantry. "If you are interested, we could venture out to see the wine cellar and the cold storage."

"You mean you have to go outside each time you need something?"

She shrugged a shoulder. "It is the smallest sacrifice, really. Other than an indoor passageway to the cellar, Monsieur Leroux's kitchen lacks for nothing."

"How far away are these rooms?"

Virginia indicated the floor. "Actually, the corridor is just below us."

Hector bent down and knocked on the floor. "Wood, not stone." He then walked the length of the pantry as if measuring each step. "Without losing much space, a staircase could be built at the back of the pantry. Perhaps I will draw up plans and show them to Gaston. He may be interested in the improvement." He chuckled. "That will give me something to do while he and Tristan and are locked in mortal combat."

When Hector thanked them and excused himself, Virginia turned to Rory. "Now. Did you really need to be present for my discussion with Hector regarding the kitchen?"

Rory sighed. "I suppose not."

He did look terribly contrite. And after what Emile had told her she took pity on Rory. "You know, I've gotten along pretty well for the past few years or so, even without your assistance."

"I know. It's just that…"

"What?" Virginia held her breath and waited for him to, at the very least, admit he cared for her.

"Well, I know how men think, that's all."

She could only stare at him. "That's all?"

"What else is there?"

Virginia wanted to scream at him. Had the man never learned how to verbalise his emotions, positive or otherwise? Then again, perhaps Emile was wrong. "Meet me here tomorrow morning at five o'clock and don't be late." With that she stomped up the stairs to her room.

* * * *

In the carriage the next morning, Virginia informed Rory that she was tired and wished to sleep the short way to the market. Their liaison in the drawing room had haunted her through the night. It was hard enough to face him remembering how she'd let her guard down, but trying to make pleasant conversation this morning with him would have been torture. Thankfully, he honoured her request and remained silent.

By now, the grocers knew what to expect when Virginia approached. She'd not had to fight for a single low price. This was due to the fact that they now respected her as a legitimate part of the culinary system, she imagined with no little amount of gratification. It was a triumph to be sure.

The vendors packed the Leroux wagon with their wares and Virginia sent it on its way, announcing to Rory that she had some private shopping to attend to.

Happily lost in her thoughts, she wandered over to an alley where a string of cloth merchants displayed their wares, thinking to look over a few items to send home for herself and Beatrice. She purchased four bolts of lovely silk brocade in a variety of colours, one striped, one floral, and two solid, an entire spool of beautiful wide black velvet ribbon for trim and no less than fifteen yards each of ivory and burgundy lace in different widths. She had the lot shipped to Beatrice's home in the United States along with a quick thank-you note to Beatrice for all her encouragement, and promising an all-day outing, just the two of them, upon Virginia's return.

As she came to the end of the row, two men took hold of her arms and pulled her into a doorway. Virginia's heart leapt into a furious beat and she prepared to unleash a hysterical scream. Covering her mouth and effectively stifling her cry for help, they dragged her through the maze of abandoned rooms until they came to the outer door on the opposite side of the building. Her eyes searched frantically for anyone who might stop her assailants, however, she found only discarded debris littering the derelict area.

They shoved her against a wall and pressed their bodies to hers. "Give us your money or you'll not see the next sunrise," one of them said in French while the other tugged at the reticule hanging from her forearm.

She yanked her elbow to and fro in order to try and keep them from ruining her empty purse. "I don't have any more money," she replied in their native tongue through the hand that covered her mouth.

"You lie. I saw how much you handed that merchant."

"Yes, I gave them all I had!"

"You'd better be wrong for your own good."

"Let her go, you bastards!"

All three of them turned toward the shouted demand. Virginia flinched with surprise and relief when she recognised Rory running toward her.

In a flash they threw her to the ground. She tumbled a few feet before she righted herself. One of them pulled out a penknife and threatened Rory with it. The fear for Rory gripped her insides and froze her blood. Her voice stalled in her throat, her lungs ceased to work as if she'd never drawn a breath in her life.

Rory picked up an arm's length piece of lead piping and brandished it at the would-be thief. The mugger lunged at Rory, but he deflected the blow, smacking the penknife out of the man's hand, who in turn began hurling debris, and anything else within his reach at Rory. His friend joined him, and Virginia was sure Rory would be pulverised by the two men.

Small metal fittings, pieces of wood with jagged, splintered edges, rocks and chunks of concrete flew towards Rory without quarter.

As if he'd practiced avoiding such blows, Rory deflected each piece of rubble with agility using the lead pipe like a sword.

Finally, Rory caught in his free hand a tangle of what looked like mangled metal trim and threw it back towards the bandits, striking one of them hard on the shoulder. The blood seeped out, a growing puddle cascading down the arm of his blue shirt.

"Fuck, let's get out of here." And as if they knew they were fighting a battle that couldn't be won, the two bandits turned and ran in the opposite direction of the markets.

He flew to her side. "Are you all right?"

Virginia could only nod.

He gathered her in his arms and held her. They didn't speak as he rocked her like a child who had awoken from a nightmare. After a while he helped her back to the carriage and settled in next to her, his arm still around her shoulders, holding her close.

It wasn't until they were halfway to the Leroux château that Virginia thanked her hero.

"Rory, my gratitude is such that I am unable to find the appropriate words…"

"Don't." He gave her a squeeze. "There is no need."

"But there is. I've foolishly pushed you away for weeks thinking I alone could take whatever situation life chose to serve me."

"What, you've never headed down an alley in a foreign country before?"

She stamped down a grin and waved a hand in dismissal of his teasing. "Today opened my eyes. I must learn to recognise when I need assistance and not be so prideful that I never ask for it. I am sorry for the way I've acted."

Rory tilted his head until their temples touched. "I, too, have been foolish. There is a place and time to trust your judgment. But I must admit, it would be quite helpful if you were to communicate with me when I seem to be uneasy."

Virginia smiled. "Consider it done. We each must rely on complete trust, and a dash of communication." He agreed with a nod, however, she knew there was one more issue between them which, if handled indelicately, would shatter like a sculpture of thinly spun sugar dropped on the floor. "There is another topic I wish to address."

"Go on."

She pulled away and turned to face him. "I need you to help keep me focused on my work. Your flirtations and such—"

"I understand perfectly. Business only, from here on out."

The sincerity in his voice alone put her at ease. She reclined against the seat with a wispy, "Thank you, Rory." Then she added, "For everything."

* * * *

"*Mon Dieu, chérie*! Someone tried to rob you? Are you all right?"

Rory had asked Emile to join him and Ginny in Monsieur Leroux's study for a briefing of their misadventure. The Leroux party wouldn't be back until supper which gave them both time to recover.

"As divine providence would have it, it was only my ego that suffered." She chuckled.

Rory would have chimed in, but he knew she was more than capable of answering Emile's questions.

Ginny continued. "The fault lies with me. It was imprudent of me to wander away from the open area."

"How much did they take from you?"

"Nothing. Rory got to me just in time. Regardless, had I relinquished my purse, they would have been sorely disappointed. I'd already spent all I had at the markets."

"And who knows how they would have taken out their displeasure on you." Emile's gaze came to rest on Rory. "Thank you, Monsieur. You are a true hero. How can we ever show you our appreciation?"

Rory felt Emile's warm gratitude in an odd way. It was almost as if the man wished to wrap his arms around him, and not in a brotherly way, either. Rory nodded. "Virginia's safety is sufficient, thanks."

All three of them headed back to the kitchen. Emile expressed once again his concern for her and she waved him off, saying she was fine now.

Only a fortnight to go before Emile left for his new job. The chef acted amicably to everyone, however, an unnamed suspicion still nagged at Rory about Ginny's friend.

Chapter Twenty

A creaking floor board caused Rory to awaken. He rolled over and turned toward the open door, only to see Emile, illuminated by the pale pre-dawn light, enter Ginny's room.

"What in the Hell..." He jumped from the bed and a warning sounded in his mind. It was Ginny's voice he heard echoing through his head, some malarkey about complete trust. *Oh, I see. My loyalty is about to undergo a test. A test that will be the death of me, or the death of Emile should it turn sour.*

Lowering himself back down to the mattress, he sat on the edge and listened. No sound came from her room, not even the murmurings of conversation through the door. What else was he to think but that they were lovers? Regardless of her denial, their behaviour pointed to that exact conclusion. Even a dimwit would be led to assume such.

Rory clenched his jaw shut. He knew Emile would be leaving today and he couldn't be happier, even though it meant that Ginny would once again take on the role of head chef. Mercifully, it wouldn't be too much longer until they boarded a ship for home.

Damnation. He sprang to his feet and prowled back and forth across the small span of the room. How long should he wait to barge in on them, three minutes? Five?

He ran a hand through his hair. Or should he wait and accost Emile when he exited?

Time had run out for Rory to try and find answers to his questions. Emile left Ginny's room and disappeared around the corner leading to the stairs.

He moved towards the door, intent on finding Emile before he left to give him a good 'what for' when he stopped short. Rory wasn't wearing a stitch of clothing. Quickly, he threw on a shirt and some trousers and ran to catch Emile.

Rory found Emile in the drive, climbing into a coach. He came to a stop at the window and peered in.

Emile smiled and lowered the window. "You surprise me, Rory, coming to say good-bye so early in the morning."

Has the man just insulted me about the fact that more than a few times, I have been late to my morning duties? Rory ignored the criticism and placed a hand on the window frame of the carriage. "I have something I'd like to say to you."

"And I to you." His smile sobered and his voice lowered, his hand coming to rest upon Rory's. "I'm sorry we didn't get to know each other better. I would have liked a more…intimate knowledge of you."

Rory's lips parted the slightest bit, but words eluded him.

"When I inquired if you would be open to it, Virginia explained that your desires were…fixed in a single direction."

Clearing his throat, Rory's voice shook, but only a little. "I...I would never have..."

"Yes, I know. Not even when I offered to take both of you to bed would she give me the least amount of hope that you would change your mind." He grinned. "It was a good thing the door to the drawing room was locked the day of your sitting. I might have joined you otherwise. The sounds of pleasure coming from that room almost sent me into a fit of passion." He gave Rory's hand a squeeze and released it. "Now, what did you wish to say?"

"Um...have a pleasant journey...and good luck."

Rory turned on his heel and strode back towards the house without another word. The echo of the gravel from under the carriage wheels bounced off the wall in front of him.

He didn't know what to think about Emile's admission. All this time, he thought Emile had been after Ginny. Without hesitation, Rory would have refused Emile, with or without Ginny in the room, her, bed.

He chuckled to himself. Hindsight told him his fears about Ginny having an affair with Emile were completely unfounded. Ginny had insisted that she and Emile were only friends. Rory understood that now.

He nearly laughed aloud. "Hell, Emile Monet is about as much of a romantic rival to me as Aunt Iris's best friend's poodle."

God, what a fool he'd been.

Rory walked around the house and glanced up at the windows on the second floor where the servant's quarters sat. The sooner he could make his intentions known the better—before the next smooth-talking Frenchie stood to make a claim for Ginny.

Inside, Madame Simone already had the kitchen whipped into a frenzy. "There you are." She approached Rory and tossed an apron to him. "I want you to knead the sourdough and let it rise. We'll need three loaves for luncheon." She indicated the corner of the kitchen where she'd set up the bowls of dough and enough flour that would likely keep him occupied for at least two hours. Disappointment got the better of him. He realised that he'd have to speak to Ginny later.

* * * *

Elbow-deep in dishwater after the Leroux party finished off the third course at supper, Rory watched his Ginny glide across the kitchen. She was a vision in her dark blue working dress. Had she jewels around her neck, she wouldn't have looked lovelier. She tied an apron to her waist while consulting with Madam Simone about the final course.

"We are ready to serve dessert, Chef Clark. I've kept it warm in one of the low-temperature ovens."

"Thank you, I appreciate your help. How long until we're ready?"

"Now is a fine time. Monsieur Hughson," Madame Simone called from across the room, "fetch the cart."

Rory wiped his hands on a nearby towel and rushed the cart over to Ginny and Madame Simone. They placed a blue porcelain platter on the cart and together they wheeled it over to the ovens.

In a combined effort, the ladies lifted the two-foot tall cone covered with Monsieur Leroux's favourite sweet cheese pastries and set it carefully in the centre of the platter.

"Hand me the sugar." Ginny nodded to Madame Simone, then took the proffered flour sifter filled with powdered sugar. She raised it above the cone and repeatedly tapped the rim, distributing a light dusting of the sugar as if it were a delicate snowfall. Handing the sifter back to Madame Simone, she turned to Rory. "Help me wheel this in, would you?"

"Of course."

Slowly they started forward, Rory pushed the teacart and Ginny held onto the cone with her thumb and forefinger.

He paused before the door to the dining room and Ginny looked up at him. The excited blush that stained her cheeks took his breath, and any other coherent thought, away. "It's beautiful."

Her smile simply beamed. "Thank you. Half of cooking is the presentation." She winked at him. "I learnt that at school. I just pray I've improved since then."

Monsieur Leroux came out of his seat when they entered. "Are those what I think they are?"

"Indeed. I made three batches for you and your guests, Monsieur."

Rory helped her place the dish in the middle of the table, then went around and distributed the dessert plates.

"Ah, *bon*! I was hoping I would have the pleasure just once more before our summer gathering came to an end!"

"There is plenty of time. I won't be leaving for another two weeks."

"Correction. You won't be leaving France, *mon chou ange*. I believe your destiny has other plans."

Antonio, Tristan and Hector chuckled. Rory went to stand next to the tea cart, pretending not to be interested in what Monsieur Leroux meant.

"I...I don't understand," she stammered and looked to the faces around the table.

"Gaston, don't keep the poor girl in suspense," Tristan said.

"Very well. Do you remember the *Pâtissier de Barbizon* competition we spoke of at the beginning of summer?"

Ginny nodded.

"As you recall, Hector suggested I sponsor you. Well, that's exactly what I did. In four days hence, the competition will take place and you, Mademoiselle Clark, are among the participants." He held up a sheaf of folded papers and handed them to her.

Rory's gaze snapped to Ginny. The blush that kissed her cheeks not moments ago had vanished. She'd turned pale as cream.

"Me?" Virginia felt her world tilt beneath her feet. "But Monsieur, I don't have time to prepare."

"You will have from tomorrow after breakfast until you depart for the competition. It should take about three hours or so. My vis-à-vis carriage will be at your disposal. Any questions you may have are likely answered in the rules." He indicated the papers with a tilt of his head.

"What about your meals? I just can't—"

"Now do not worry yourself. I have arranged for the three of us," he indicated his guests, "and a small portion of my household to go ahead of you. A few nights in the Hotel Barbizon will be a fitting end to our summer party, no?" He winked at Antonio, Tristan and Hector, then returned his attention to

Virginia. "You will have plenty of time to create that way. In addition, you have the rest of my house to see to your needs, including your kitchen staff. You don't mind being left in charge of my château, do you?" He chuckled.

Virginia shook her head, but Tristan interrupted what would have been another protest. "Gaston has placed a hundred thousand francs on you to win."

When she began to choke, Rory stepped up to pat her on the back.

"Thank you," she murmured to him just after recovering.

Chapter Twenty-One

Not long after Monsieur Leroux left, Virginia sat at one end of the kitchen staring at a sketch pad Antonio had given her and chewing on the end of a pencil Tristan had parted with in support of her effort. The rules sat in her pocket, the paper wrinkled and worn having been read over and over in order for Virginia to memorise each regulation.

Certain that sweet pastries had been done before in French Pâtissier contests, she longed to create something different for this competition, something that would travel well, and not need to be kept warm, or on fire, when served. Perhaps her creation could symbolise a celebration of the human spirit. It needed to be spectacular, to stand out above the crowd. It would have to be tall, but not cone-shaped, everything statuesque seemed to be attached to a cone and she wanted her entry to be unique.

A giggle bubbled up from between her lips as she envisioned a foot-tall petit-four. Then all at once she froze. A wedding cake! But how could she make it different, more interesting than what the cooking academy taught her was popular?

Virginia's imagination took over and the pencil glided across the paper before her. Soon a three-tiered wedding cake adorned the page in glorious charcoal and white. "This needs flowers." She added a cascade of petit-four flowers that spilt down the side as if the goddess of spring herself had planted them there.

Adding a few notes on her page, she thought to hide quarter-inch-thick hardened sugar disks beneath each of the two top layers for stability, split all three cakes in half lengthwise and add a buttery vanilla-rum filling between layers. A stroke of genius, it was, and she didn't mind saying so.

* * * *

"*Mon dieu*," Madame Simone declared with a mouthful of test cake that evening after supper. "I've never tasted anything better. You will win the contest for sure."

Rory couldn't speak. A combination of awe and butter-rum filling were the culprits. Ginny turned to him for his reaction, but all he could do was nod in agreement with Madame Simone.

She gave him an adorable smile. "I was hoping you'd like it. I haven't created a dessert from a drawing since my finals at cooking school."

With a finger, Ginny scooped up a dollop of filling and popped it between her plump lips. It would be the death of Rory if she continued to tempt him in this way. If there was one thing that fuelled his fire, it was watching her sample things. He loved the way her finger slid into her mouth, the way she sucked the taste from her long, slim digit. He'd endured it all summer long, but he was positive he'd never get used to the feelings her tiny action provoked. If he had his druthers, he'd drag her back to the damned drawing room floor and… He shook himself mentally and searched the kitchen counter to change the subject. Finding one, he swallowed. "The flowers are—"

"Yes, I know," she interrupted him. "I didn't replicate my drawing exactly. Really I just wanted to sample all three tastes together, the cake, the filling and the icing. Besides, I can't possibly assemble the cake until I get there, the journey in a carriage over who knows what sort of road wouldn't permit it."

"Have you thought about how you will transport the cakes?"

She shook her head. "Actually, no. I didn't want to think about it until I knew for sure what my presentation would consist of."

"Don't you worry about it." Rory placed his hand upon her warm shoulder. "We'll figure out how to convey the items safely tomorrow morning. We are, after all, ahead of schedule." When Ginny smiled at him, his heart practically melted in his chest. She seemed so vulnerable at that moment. Rory would've done anything to protect her and her interests. Absentmindedly, he tucked a stray lock of hair behind her ear. She blushed and looked away as if unable to meet his gaze. He hoped she, too, wished they were the only two people on Earth. Rory stifled a sigh. Likely it wouldn't be until they returned home that he could sit down and have a serious discussion with her about their future, provided a future for them existed.

* * * *

"Mademoiselle! Mademoiselle!"

Virginia heard Madam Simone calling her from all the way inside the pantry. She set down the sugar crock and followed the sound. Madame Simone, who'd been benevolently assisting Virginia, stood before the oven where the cake for the competition lay baking.

"What is it, Madam Sim—"

"Your cake! It has fallen!"

"What?" Virginia peered into the open oven door. "Oh, no!" In the centre of the cake sat a great indentation as deep as a bloody well. Her stomach mimicked the sight before her. She could have doubled over from the pain.

"You'll have to start all over now. Quick, I will clean and dry the cooking implements and you gather the ingredients."

"Y...yes, of course." Virginia turned toward the pantry and promptly went blank. She stood there, helpless, her mind going in five different directions at once. Had she measured all the ingredients properly? Had she added something she shouldn't have or forgotten anything? What if it happened again? She wouldn't have anything to enter into the contest...

From behind, she heard her name, soft as a breeze, and yet was unable to move.

"Ginny? I heard what happened. Are you all right?"

She swallowed, still frozen to the spot.

"You've been working very hard for over twenty-four hours now. Come, sit with me for a moment. I had an idea."

Virginia allowed Rory to guide her to a pair of stools set before the large butcher's block in the centre of the kitchen. She barely noticed Madame Simone at the sink scrubbing away.

Rory kneaded her shoulders from behind and spoke in soothing tones. "I have an idea about how to transfer the cakes to the competition."

She took a shuddering breath. "Provided they don't fall again."

"They won't. I promise." She felt his hands slide to her upper arms. The warmth served to melt the sheet of ice surrounding her. "The cake falling was a stroke of bad luck, that's all. You made the cake perfectly before, you will do it again." He gave her a gentle squeeze—almost, but not quite a hug.

"I don't have much time left—we leave first thing in the morning. What if..."

"Now." He stepped around to stand before her. "You mustn't think like that. We must move forward. All right?"

Virginia finally met his gaze. He was looking at her so tenderly that she wanted nothing more than to fall into his arms and stay there until they returned home to the States. She shouldn't be thinking in this direction, but she desperately needed his touch, for more reasons than she could count.

"Good. Now, in cold storage, I found Monsieur Leroux's Veuve Clicquot trunk—"

"The order Madame Simone sent to the winery has not arrived yet."

"I know, and I think this will be to our advantage."

"H...how so?"

"What if we filled the bottom with ice and set the cakes, still in their pans inside the well-padded, suspended tray? It is what normally keeps the champagne bottles from being jostled about, why shouldn't it work for us?"

She paused and envisioned his idea.

He smiled. "Then no matter how bad the roads turn out to be, the layers would be cushioned."

"Not only that but the cool, humid air from the ice would keep the cake moist." Snapping out of her ill humour, she added, "Oh, Rory. You are a genius!" She jumped from the stool with rekindled purpose and headed for the pantry. "Madame Simone, let's have those bowls and pans as soon as you are finished!" she tossed over her shoulder.

* * * *

Virginia could sense the inner calm before the storm, and not because the clouds hung low and heavy in the sky above. She'd got a decent night's sleep after the cakes came out of the oven in a perfect state. Presently, she and Rory sat inside the carriage having vacated their rooms and loaded their baggage. She'd said goodbye to Madame Simone and the remaining household staff who had turned up to wish her the best of luck.

Every last ingredient she needed for the competition had been set into the wagon with the rest of the items that would follow them to their destination. Rory suggested that the filling be premixed and set amongst the ice to save time, and for that stroke of brilliance Virginia was grateful. The drivers had their instructions.

She was brought out of her musings when Rory chuckled from the seat across from her. "I can see you ticking off the 'to do' list in your mind."

"I don't want to forget a single thing." She blew out a breath. "Do you suppose it's too much to beg perfection of the universe just this once?"

"Not at all. I'm most certain Divine Providence will comply for the 'Angel of Pastry'."

With a loud pop, the carriage lurched forward and she giggled with relief. Everything she had worked for since the beginning of the summer boiled down to this one competition. This would be the final word, before the entire community of French...

"Did you hear that odd sound?" Rory murmured and sat forward, gazing out of the window toward the Leroux Château. "What on earth...?"

A sinking feeling settled in her stomach as if it had been there all along waiting for the right moment to make itself known. Alarmed, Virginia turned to see what he was looking at.

A wide pillar of black smoke billowed into the air from behind the house. She then noticed Madame Simone running toward the carriage, waving her arms and shouting.

Rory tossed open the door and shouted. "Stop the carriage!" He jumped down and helped Virginia alight.

"Mademoiselle! The kitchen—" Madame Simone gasped. "It's on fire!"

Stepping forward, Rory took over. "Who is putting it out?"

"Everyone, Monsieur."

Rory nodded and his gaze met Virginia's. "You can't go back."

"I must. I've been left in charge and—"

"They can handle it."

"But I have to be sure." She turned towards the house when he stopped her.

"What about the competition? If we don't leave now, we won't make check-in."

"I cannot waste time arguing about this with you."

"Very well." He forced out a frustrated sigh. "I suppose it shouldn't take long to put out a fire."

She was positive her stated gratitude was lost as she was already running for the house alongside Madame Simone. She knew that Rory was right behind them, but didn't take the time to turn and look.

The smoke poured out through the back door so thickly that the household servants were unable to use the water from the kitchen tap. Rory joined a bucket brigade of at least ten people that stretched from the nearest fountain to the doors of the cold storage and wine cellar. With a lump in her stomach the size of a melon, Virginia could see the flames eating away at Monsieur Leroux's beautiful home.

"The fire began in this area. Pray it stays here," Madame Simone shouted above the noise of Monsieur Leroux's servants who worked to put out the fire.

"How'd it start?"

"A gas pipe leading to one of the ovens broke."

"Oh, God. And they've been turned off since?"

"*Oui*, and the main shut-off valve is secure. I could not bear another explosion."

She stifled a groan. "No one was hurt?"

"No. There was no one in the kitchen at the time."

Virginia nodded and took up a bucket.

Chapter Twenty-Two

Finally, white smoke gave way to steam as the water hit the last of the smouldering embers, dousing the heat.

Rory stood behind her as she gazed at the remains. His hands came to rest upon her shoulders. "Listen, now that I know you are safe, I'll see that you are entered into the contest and I'll set everything up in your assigned area." He turned her to face him. "Are you listening?"

She nodded.

"I understand how important this is to you, Ginny, and I also know that you'd regret it for the rest of your life if you were to miss this opportunity."

Even if Virginia thought that he was wrong, she didn't have the strength to argue with him right now.

"As soon as you feel you can leave the château, get on a horse, then ride like Hell to the other side of Barbizon. One of the groomsmen here, I'm sure, would be happy to escort you."

"I will try."

He placed his cool hand upon her heated cheek. "And I will look for you at every moment."

It seemed as if he was about to kiss her, but he slid his hand from her face and strode away. Pity, because she could have used a kiss right about now.

Just before he turned the corner for the front of the house he looked back at her. "Don't be long, love." Then he was gone.

She turned back to the rubble. The doors and ceiling to the cellar and over half of the pantry were now non-existent. The entire wall, including the hall which led to the servant's quarters and most of the pantry ceiling were but a memory, leaving a gaping hole in the side of the house. They'd lost the items in the pantry that hadn't been consumed by fire to smoke and water damage. Many of Monsieur Leroux's wine bottles were broken or undrinkable from heat exposure and the cold storage was no longer cold.

Virginia walked through the smoky, half-gutted kitchen and sighed. She came to a stop at the edge of the pantry.

"Do not get too close, Mademoiselle. The floor is unstable," Madame Simone said from behind Virginia.

"You mean what's left of it."

"*Oui.*"

Madame Simone patted her on the arm and left to see to the exhausted servants. Virginia buried her face into her hands. What would she say to Monsieur Leroux? He'd be angry for certain that his house had been left in the hands of an incompetent fool. No, it wasn't all her fault, but she still felt the gravity of the situation upon her shoulders for the kitchen burnt while she was in charge.

Not so distant thunder pulled her from her foreboding thoughts. The situation would surely be worsened if…

A single, fat raindrop landed on the floor in front of her, followed by another, then another.

"My God," she whispered. "After the flood shall we expect a plague of flies?"

* * * *

It was a bitter sort of irony that the buckets which were used earlier in the day to quench an angry fire's flames were the same buckets that now hauled rain water out of the corridor of the decrepit wine cellar and dilapidated cold storage. It could be assumed, by the total darkness Virginia and the rest of the staff worked in, that the sun had long since set. The rain continued to pour mercilessly down upon the helpless lot.

Virginia didn't even want to know what the state of the rest of the kitchen dwelt in. Damnation, it hadn't rained this hard all summer long. She couldn't even think about how the weather was affecting Rory's journey. Any minute now he'd come slogging through the mud back to the château, and Monsieur Leroux would be out not only the small fortune he'd wagered on her for the pastry competition, but the mountain of money he'd have to spend repairing his home.

Madame Simone called down to Virginia from the pantry above. "We've just received word that construction workers will be here as early as first light to assess the damage. If the weather cooperates, that is."

Virginia nodded her thanks.

* * * *

Just as dawn broke, golden light seeped through the window sheers of Monsieur Leroux's study. Virginia stood in the centre of the room, finally in a dry, serviceable, dark brown wool dress, borrowed from one of the house maids. She was certain that if she sat down, she'd never get up again.

"Mademoiselle?" Madame Simone entered with a steaming cup of tea and handed it to Virginia.

"Where did you find this?" Virginia asked with a raspy voice then took a healing sip.

"It is my own personal tea." She shrugged.

Virginia managed a smile. "But you are French. I had no idea you drank tea."

"We all have our vices."

Had Virginia's throat not ached from shouting communications for at least fourteen hours straight, she would have laughed. "Again, thank you. You've been so wonderful this entire summer."

Madame Simone waved away the compliment. "I've sent a wagon and two of the servers to the markets for a few essentials. You should try and get some rest, Mademoiselle."

"How can I when the pastry competition has started without me?"

"I thought it started at noon today?"

"Noon is when the judging begins."

"Then you have a few hours."

At the moment, Virginia hadn't the wit to argue. "I suppose I could go if only to see who wins. I'll have to speak to Monsieur Leroux about his kitchen at some point and it may as well be sooner rather than later."

A knock interrupted them. "Chef Clark?" One of the house servants peered in through the door. "The construction men have arrived."

"Very well." Virginia turned toward the door. "I'll just..."

"No. I cannot let you meet them, you are exhausted. A rest will do you much good. I shall speak with the workers." Madame Simone took Virginia by the arm over to the fainting couch in the corner. "In the meantime, you are to lie down here." She unfolded a small blanket and placed it over Virginia. "I will let you know when they have finished assessing the damage."

Without a word of protest, Virginia complied—her eyes closing the instant Madame Simone and the servant exited the room.

* * * *

What seemed like the blink of an eye later, but had been in actuality two full hours according to the mantel clock, Madame Simone re-entered the study. "Mademoiselle Clark, the construction workers are about to leave. They say it will be a few days before plans can be drawn up to replace the burnt sections."

"A few days?" Virginia stood feeling far more refreshed than she had when she first laid her head down. However, panic quickly replaced her rejuvenation. "But what if it rains again? What if..." Hector's project! She took a step toward Madame Simone. "Plans, you say? The workers need to obtain plans before they can move forward?"

"*Oui.*"

"We have them—somewhere. Quick, help me search Monsieur Leroux's desk." She went around and reached for the main drawer, pulling it open. "In a moment of boredom, Hector came to the kitchen and designed a staircase from the back of the pantry to the cellars." She moved a few papers around in the drawer as she searched. "If we can find it, the workers can use that as a starting point and perhaps put some sort of temporary roof up." Yanking open another drawer, she shuffled around in it. "I know it's here somewhere, it has to be."

Madame Simone drew Virginia's attention to a sketch she lifted from atop the desk. "Could this be it?"

Virginia took the proffered page. "Yes, that's it. Quick, run and stop them from leaving. Tell them they have the beginnings of the kitchen right here."

Madame Simone didn't hesitate. She scurried off to do as bid.

Invigorated and ready to face her fate head on, Virginia folded the blanket and exited the study.

After exploring the remains of what used to be the centre work area of the kitchen, she met Madame Simone just outside the back door and witnessed the reconstruction already in progress.

"We are lucky, Mademoiselle. They had leftover lumber from their last job."

Virginia agreed with a nod. "Are you sure you will be all right if I go?"

"I've already called for a horse for you and Jean, Monsieur Leroux's head groom, is ready to escort you to the competition. Now, I insist you take your leave before you miss everything."

There was still so much to be done in the kitchen, but she had full confidence in Madame Simone. "You've been so...so...oh, how can I express my gratitude?"

"Mademoiselle Clark, you have shown me more respect and kindness than a superior of mine has ever granted me. However, if you don't depart right this instant, I'll have Jean bully you into leaving."

Virginia couldn't help but laugh. She held up her hands in surrender. "All right, all right, I'm going."

Jean came round the house with two horses and waved Virginia over.

"I apologise for not having a lady's saddle, Mademoiselle."

"Monsieur, I grew up in Tombstone. I wouldn't know a lady's saddle if it introduced itself to me." With that she swung up onto the horse in one fluid motion.

As Jean mounted his horse, Virginia heard Madame Simone chuckle. "Is there nothing she cannot do?"

Virginia turned to Madame Simone. "Believe me, the list of things I can do is much shorter than the list of things I cannot."

The older woman smiled. "From what I've witnessed, every day you live on this earth you prove that theory wrong."

Heat suffused Virginia's cheeks. "You are too kind, Madame Simone. *Au revoir*."

Jean pulled his horse alongside Virginia's. "If we ride due east at a decent pace and the roadway isn't too muddy, we should be there in under an hour."

"Thank you, Jean, now try to keep up." She chuckled.

As he grinned, Virginia dug her heels into the flanks of the horse. "Yah!"

Chapter Twenty-Three

They were a mud-splotched mess by the time they'd reached the address of the competition. Jean took the horses round back to rub them down and allow them to rest a bit before heading back. After Virginia quickly rinsed her hands and face in a fountain just outside the entrance, she tried in vain to wipe the damp dirt clumps from her skirt. Giving up, she cautiously stepped through the doors.

Quiet murmurings tickled her ears and she settled into a chair at the back of the room. The fact that the seat wasn't bounding down a road in the French countryside she counted as a blessing. It was a smallish room, only about twenty-five or so people made up the audience. To her left and in the very front row sat Monsieur Leroux and his party of artists. Rory sat to the right in the second row, staring straight ahead as if in a trance. She hoped he wasn't too upset with her for abandoning the contest.

Upon a low stage, a table stretched along the front of the room which featured the entries. A spun-sugar sculpture of a tree from which real cherries dangled sat at one end of the table. Next was a tall cone of glazed plums and apricots. A ceramic bowl topped with a flaky, puffed pastry shell came after that, then a mountain of what looked like little mauve icing flowers took centre stage. Of the three remaining dishes, the only one she recognised was berries threaded with curling ribbons of what must have been meringue, the others she couldn't tell what they were. One might have been a chocolate mousse, but in the low light, it was hard to tell. One thing for sure, her cake hadn't made it to the final stage.

She exhaled a sigh and sat back in her chair when a man came to stand before the desserts. "*Messieurs et mesdames*, we have gathered the judge's tallies and here are the results of our contest." He set his spectacles atop his nose and looked down at the paper in his other hand. "In third place, Chef Remy St Vincent's Chocolate Mousse."

The crowd politely clapped.

"In second place, Chef Jean-Pierre Pope's Brandied Berries a la meringue."

Again the crowd applauded softly.

"In first place, Chef Frederique De Leon's Cherry Tree."

The crowd applauded again, but quieted down when the man raised his hand.

"In the final category, ladies and gentlemen, with unprecedented high scores not only in taste and presentation but originality as well, our Sweepstakes winner, along with five hundred francs, goes to…" He glanced down at his paper and grinned. "Chef Virginia Clark's Wedding Cake."

The crowd came to its feet in audible jubilation,. Virginia must have heard wrong. Her cake was nowhere to be seen, however, the man had announced her name. Slowly Virginia stood and made her way to Rory. She waited until the group of men including Monsieur Leroux and his party finished congratulating him, then stepped forward.

Rory was the first to notice her. He pulled her into a rough embrace. "You made it."

"Barely. But I don't understand. How..."

"I'll explain later. Right now you must face your public."

Each in turn, Antonio, Hector, Tristan and Monsieur Leroux kissed Virginia's cheeks.

"You've made me a small fortune, *mon chou ange.*" Monsieur Leroux opened his left lapel and there, sticking out of the pocket of his waistcoat, sat a plump envelope.

His ten thousand francs. Virginia grinned bashfully. "It hardly seems I've done anything at all to deserve this honour." She glanced at Rory then returned her attention to Monsieur Leroux. "I must beg a moment of your time. You see..."

The announcer interrupted the group. "Ah, so this must be Chef Clark."

Reluctantly, Virginia faced him. "I am, Monsieur."

"*Bon.* The judges wish to meet you. Right this way."

She followed him over to the table upon the stage praying they didn't notice her mussed dress. Silently she thanked the heavens for the absence of windows in the room.

Virginia acknowledged the judges' praise, but her focus was on the cake before her. It stood about as tall as her test cake, but where the dozens upon dozens of perfect little violet-mauve icing flowers came from, she had no clue.

After the judges handed her a certificate of Sweepstakes and her five hundred francs, Monsieur

Leroux came over to claim the rest of the cake, telling them it was his finder's fee for sending them Chef Clark. Then he announced to Virginia, Rory and his party that dinner was his treat tonight at the Hotel Barbizon.

While Antonio carried the cake and Tristan and Hector gave him opposing instructions on how not to drop it, Rory occasionally glanced over his shoulder, watching as Virginia and Monsieur Leroux trailed at a slight distance.

"There is no other way to say this, Monsieur, so I'll just come out with it. Your kitchen has been terribly damaged due to a fire." She added hastily, "The rain didn't help matters, either."

"Wha—?"

"I'm so sorry. It is my understanding that there was a gas leak."

"*Mon Dieu*, was anyone hurt?"

"No, thank Heavens. But the destruction…the cost…"

"Don't you worry yourself over it." He patted her back reassuringly. "I'll have it put to rights when I return."

Virginia's shoulders felt lighter than they had in days. "Thank you, Monsieur, for not being angry with me."

"Did you yourself light the kitchen on fire?"

She grinned. "Of course not."

"Then there is no reason for me to be upset with you." He pulled her close and placed a fatherly kiss upon her temple.

* * * *

The party changed for dinner. Rory had allowed Virginia privacy in his room where her trunks had been stored. She'd think about procuring her own room later. After she'd taken a hot bath, put on one of her own dresses and re-pinned her hair in a simple chignon, she made her way down to the hotel dining room.

Once they were seated, she told everyone about the kitchen fire and flood.

"Madame Simone," she turned to Monsieur Leroux, "to whom I owe a great debt of gratitude for all her help, found Hector's plans for the stair case he'd drawn up for the pantry. She gave his sketch and notes to the construction workers and they started right away on the project."

Monsieur Leroux laughed. "Ah, Hector, I knew you would come in handy one of these days."

Hector feigned insult. "I won't allow you to forget to pay me for my work, Gaston."

He chuckled. "No need to worry, Hector." He reached into the envelope in his pocket. "Here is twenty francs." The party chuckled at Monsieur Leroux's antics.

"Ha! A paltry sum for a project of *mine*."

"You are right, *mon ami*. Twenty now and five more when it is complete."

The Leroux party, finding their host's dry humour riveting, laughed at his quip.

While the artists bantered on with each other, an arm snaked around Virginia. Who else could it be but the wonderful, benevolent man she'd adored practically since young adulthood? Rory pulled her close. "As amusing as these Frenchmen are," he whispered, "I can't wait to get you alone."

The very thought of she and Rory alone made Virginia's heart leap within her chest. Now that her summer employment was officially at an end, she supposed she could afford herself a tiny bit of recreation. As tired as she was, the evening loomed before her, but she should at least pretend to play her 'hard to get' card. "Yes, well, who knows when that will be?" She ignored the fact that her breathless voice betrayed her emotions.

"I know exactly when it will be. I have my room for one more night and, as I'm sure you noticed, the bed is far too big for me alone."

She tried to shift away from him and make it look like it was for decorum's sake but her semi-good intentions turned out to be unsuccessful.

His arm felt so wonderfully strong, encircling her body the way he was. "And what makes you think you can tempt me again, Mr Hughson?"

"Oh, the fact that your blush is at a rolling boil and," he leaned in even closer. "I can sense your anticipation."

Virginia laughed woodenly and pushed his meddling hands from her sensitised person. He wasn't making playing coy very easy. "You'll be lucky if I can stay awake through dessert," she whispered, although he couldn't have called her inner turmoil better.

Virginia's prize-winning cake arrived for the dessert course, missing only the sliver used in the judging.

Rory's seductive teasing had been fanning her fires for at least an hour. Now it was time to change the subject. "Rory, I insist you tell us how the flowers came to be that fascinating mauve colour," she said as a hotel server cut and served the cake.

The Leroux party encouraged his story as well.

He gave her a sidelong glance as if he knew her ploy. He cleared his throat. "Once it was assembled, I noted that at a distance, one couldn't distinguish the white flowers from the white background. I searched around to find something that would tint the icing, when I happened upon some left-over blackberries from luncheon."

"You used blackberry juice? That's nothing short of genius," Virginia said in earnest awe. "But why so much?" she asked and took a bite. The ensemble along with the added flavour was quite delicious, she had to admit.

"Well, that's where my mistake nearly overtook me. At first I used too little juice for the amount of icing I had. Then I used too much. I had to add more confectioners' sugar and soon I had enough icing for three cakes. So I piped the flowers onto the white icing and before I knew it, the entire cake was covered."

"So your triumph was, in essence, born of error?" Monsieur Leroux asked with a mouth full of cake.

Rory grinned. "More or less."

"You should have put your name in the contest instead of mine," Virginia half-joked.

"Chef Clark," Rory announced formally. "The wedding cake was your idea. You came up with the design, baked the cakes, created the filling and taught me to pipe icing flowers. It was only right that you should get the credit." His blue eyes skimmed over her and she felt a shiver run up her spine.

Finished with his piece of cake, Monsieur Leroux leaned in toward Virginia and Rory and waggled his eyebrows. "He deserves a hero's reward, eh, Mademoiselle?"

Virginia could feel her blush creeping all the way from her toes to her temples while each man at the table, including Rory, lifted their glasses in agreement.

Just then, everyone's attention was diverted to the front door. About a dozen giggling young French women filed into the room, searching for a table big enough to accommodate their party.

"Look at the time," Tristan indicated the grandfather clock against the wall.

"I think I'll stretch my legs," Antonio murmured and stood.

Hector grinned. "I think I know that girl."

"Which one?" Monsieur Leroux inquired.

"That one." He pointed then retracted his hand. "No, not that one. Any one. Does it matter?"

"*Bon*. I shall require an introduction."

"To which one?"

"Any one. Does it matter?"

Virginia smiled. "Monsieur Leroux," she called from her seat. He turned and closed the small distance between them. "Please take the rest of the cake. It should make a fine conversation piece."

"I shall. *Au revoir, mon chou ange.*"

"Expect the return of your carriage tomorrow evening. Thank you for everything, Monsieur Leroux."

He kissed the top of her head and carried the cake over to where Antonio, Hector and Tristan were already getting cosy with the group of women.

A great sigh escaped from deep within her chest. She hadn't got in trouble for the kitchen fire and she'd actually won the top prize in a French pastry contest. It was one of those moments in life where everything seemed perfect.

Confident she could have any type of kitchen job available in Europe or the States, she stood.

"Where are you off to?"

She hadn't noticed, but Rory had also stood and pulled out her chair. She thought fast. "I'm going to secure a room for myself at the front desk."

"You can't."

"And why is that?"

"Um, this hotel is all sold out."

"How do you know?"

He paused in his banter with her. She could see in his eyes there were thoughts churning in his mind. "Well, it will be when I reserve every last room in my name."

Silently, Virginia considered it a possibility that she'd won the heart of this man, game, set and match. She folded her arms across her chest. "Why on Earth...no. I know exactly why you would do such a thing. You would go through the time and expense just so that I would have to sleep in your room, wouldn't you?"

He took her by the upper arms and pulled her close. "That's one of the things I love most about you."

Unable to quell her victorious trembling, likely because she was so tired, she squared her shoulders. "Care to finish that thought, sir?"

"You're intelligent."

His breath tickled the hair at her forehead and she chuckled. Life couldn't have served up a more blissful circumstance than what the end of this day offered, and she was more than ready to indulge in the fare before her. She'd chastise herself for giving into her wanton side tomorrow. Right now, as she stood dangerously close to the man who held her heart in the palm of his hand, she sighed and leaned her forehead against his chin in surrender. "I am officially too tired to bandy words with you."

"Excellent. Then I shall throw you over my shoulder and, like some randy barbarian, carry you up the stairs."

He wouldn't dare. She pulled away enough to look into his eyes. "You'll have to kill me first. There are some lines a lady doesn't cross."

He leered at her, that Hughson dimple taunting her. "In public, you mean."

The rumble in his voice caused heat to surround her body in a sensual bubble. She drew a breath to ask what he'd meant by that when he released her and took up his yet untouched slice of cake.

"What's that for?" she breathed, almost sure his intentions were licentious.

"To sweeten the deal." With one final glance at the Leroux party, Rory snaked his arm around her waist and ushered her out of the dining area and up the stairs to his room.

Chapter Twenty-Four

Rory shut the door behind them and set the cake upon a chest of drawers. Already the serpent between his legs, hard and hot for Ginny, pressed against the closure of his trousers. He watched her at the window as she parted the drapes on the other side of the room.

"Waiting for someone?" he asked and lit a lamp upon the night stand.

"I was just thinking."

"About?" Tossing the spent match aside, he lowered the flame, bringing the light in the room to a warm, seductive glow.

She let the sheers close but kept the heavy curtains apart. From over her shoulder he could see that the moon was up, shining over the French countryside. "About my wonderful time here in France."

He made his way over to her. "Before or after you battled the fire?"

Her laugh sounded choked. "Well, aside from that part. The summer was just perfect, Rory, and I have you to thank. I couldn't have conquered half the battles had you not helped me."

"It was, without a doubt, the most interesting summer I've had," he murmured and slid his hands around her waist from behind.

"Ever?"

"Mmm-hm." Rory buried his nose into her hair and inhaled. He'd know her scent anywhere, all earth and feminine and…Ginny.

She turned in his arms. "I'm surprised to hear you say that after all the time spent at your Aunt Iris'."

"I can honestly say I'd never cleaned and dressed dozens of fowl, piped petite icing flowers onto cakes and been pursued by another man before in my entire life. Being party to such happenings, madam, would make any venture interesting."

Ginny giggled, the sound vibrated the muscles in his arms. "All that was my fault." Regret, feigned or not, rang in her voice.

"I wouldn't have had it any other way."

She leaned against him in response. He wrapped his arms around her and gave her squeeze. Then he deftly began unhooking the back of her simple gown. The woman before him should be draped in silks. He'd see to that later. He drew the fabric down her thighs and it pooled at her ankles. Now for her underpinnings. He couldn't wait to run his hands along her smooth skin, up her arms, down her back, up her legs…

Dressed in only her corset, drawers, stockings and slippers, Ginny stepped over her dress and away from him. "May I have a moment?"

With his head swimming round and round like a large fish in a small bowl, Rory agreed and allowed her privacy in the wash room of his suite. She turned away and he ran his hands down his face. As much as he'd accused her of a heated blush earlier, it was in fact, he who might as well have been a nervous, green groom.

Seconds before she shut the door, she gave him a look that he hadn't seen since that damn day in that damn carriage. Damn that day indeed. It was that day by which every other woman he'd met, every other kiss he'd shared, was measured. Not a single girl, confessed professional or otherwise, could compare to his Ginny.

And after that day in Leroux's study, he didn't want anyone else in his bed.

No one.

Just Ginny.

Forever.

In a daze Rory shed his waistcoat, shirt and boots, and reached for his dressing robe. He slipped his arms through, but before he could tie the front closed, the door to his washroom opened. She walked toward him, a drying towel wrapped around her lush body.

She hoped her wrung-out hands didn't look as bloodless as they felt as she clutched the fabric to her chest. She wanted him, badly, and knew it had shown on her face not a few moments ago. But she felt desperate not to appear as she did when they were adolescents, needy, impulsive...randy. Perhaps it was about time she became the perfect lady, even when she stood naked in front of the man she was about to hop between the sheets with, the only man with whom she would do such a thing, regardless of the fact that he still hadn't offered for her. And that was where her error lay. She'd lost her heart to him long ago but for him, she was just a distraction from real life. At least, that was how it felt.

The day of the art sitting had been altogether different, too. He'd seduced her. Now here they were and this time, the decision to indulge seemed to come from both of them and it felt awkward. There was no possible way she'd say no to him, but what was the decent way to say yes? Certainly not the way she'd conducted herself at the sitting. Had they been man and wife, things would be different. Much different. She wouldn't feel the need for permission, she could ride Rory the Wild Pony any time she wanted to, night after night if it pleased her. She nearly smiled, but that odd uncertainty sneaked in and stole her grin away. Ladies didn't think things like that.

Lured back to the situation before her, she blinked as he held out his hand to her. "What's wrong?"

This was not the best time for her emotions to show on her face. She let go of the towel and took his hand with her free one. "N…nothing."

He drew her to him and reached up, tilting her face so that her eyes met his gaze. "I know that look. Now out with it."

Her lips parted, but no words emerged.

"Are you still worried about the damage to Monsieur Leroux's château?"

"No, it's not that."

"Then what?" His hand slipped from her chin.

She turned her face away, unable to look into his eyes. "After everything I've learned, all the schooling I've been through, I still find it difficult to conduct myself like a lady. I'm lustful and wanton and use filthy words when I'm under your spell. I crave your nearness and when you aren't there, all I can think about is you. Have you any idea how many times I pushed passionate thoughts of you and I away this summer?" She looked back into his eyes, hoping his reaction wasn't something akin to repulsed. Instead, his gaze raked hotly over her person.

"Ginny, if I wanted a lady in my bedroom, I'd have married one of those southern chits my aunt threw at me."

"Wha—?"

"You are fire and ice, perfection at both temperatures and in between. You tease me with your eyes and body, do and say things that make me lose my mind."

"I do not...well, at least not at every moment of the day."

"Indeed you do. I can tell what you're thinking sometimes when you don't know I'm watching you and it's almost always naughty."

She made to protest further when he drew her over to the bed and bid her to sit. He slid the robe from his shoulders. The sight of his naked torso nearly knocked the breath from her. Then he took up his slice of cake. "Go on. Test the filling." He held it out to her.

She looked at him, searching his eyes for an ounce of sanity.

"Come on. Just the way you do in the kitchen."

Shrugging, she dipped a finger into the cake and popped it into her mouth.

Rory groaned aloud and set the plate down on the bed next to her.

She sucked on the tip of her finger. "What?" she asked with a dollop of sweet cream on her tongue.

"I've watched you do that all summer long." Deftly he stripped himself of his trousers then pressed her back onto the pile of pillows that sat against the headboard. "Do you have any idea what that does to me?" he said in a ragged voice.

Virginia swallowed and shook her head.

He reached over, stuck a finger in the cake.

Her eyes widened as he wiped the icing onto her nipple.

"I want to smother you in custard." His voice lowered to almost a growl. "I want to pipe tiny flowers all over your body and suck every single one of them off."

She felt like swooning at his words. Virginia's head fell back onto the pillow, her breath held. He bent his head to her breast and licked until the icing was gone.

All ideas of social grandeur flew out of the window. After what seemed like a very long moment, she spoke. "Rory, that is so...so..."

"I know. Bad. Evil. I should be ashamed—"

Her head came up. "No. It's so... *Indecent*." She whispered the description.

"I'm so sorry. I..."

"No, you mistake me." Overcome with lust, she scooped up half the cake and smeared it between her legs. "I want more," she wheezed and heard the breath leave his lungs.

She licked the palm of her hand from wrist to the tip of her middle finger, then smeared the head of his thick, engorged manhood with cake and frosting.

It was more than he could stand. He manoeuvred next to her on the bed, and rolled her onto her side facing him, his face at the juncture of her thighs. "Take my cock into your mouth."

When she did, his entire body buzzed with sensation. The sucking sounds she made could have been his undoing, however, before him sat the most delicious dessert he'd ever been served, better than any pastry in that damn contest.

He took her by the hips and his mouth came down on her. She ceased her sucking, but only for a moment. With a groan she continued, licking him, drawing him deeply down her throat.

No cotillion picnic or brandy at midnight had ever been this tasty, no assigned task on earth this stimulating.

She was almost clean when she shattered between his hands, convulsing and moaning, almost shouting his name. If he didn't pull away now he'd come in her mouth. *She probably wouldn't mind, either, the little vixen.* He almost smiled. But Rory didn't want this to end. No, he was going to pleasure her all night long. This was the first time she was his for the entire night, and sleep was not on the menu, although he might permit a few five minute intervals here and there. He drew back, righted himself and settled his cock between her thighs.

"I need to get inside you, Ginny love. Your sweet pussy, it seems, is begging me to take you."

She lifted her knee next to his chest and with a husky voice purred, "Fuck me until I die."

Rory plunged into her and her vocals began again until they rose greater than before. She was singing his name once more, her inner muscles gripping and sliding over his penis in frantic spasms.

"My Ginny." He slammed into her. "Mine." He increased his tempo, hardened his thrusts, holding his pleasure back, elongating her orgasm, drawing multiples from her, until at last the stars behind his eyes exploded. He poured himself, his love, his life force into her as he pressed home between her soaked thighs.

Her body, still clenching his, began to relax, her whimpers and hitched breaths twitched in sync with her slick channel. Reluctantly, he rolled from her and settled close.

Their breathing nearing normal, she turned and draped an arm over his chest. "Rory. That was…"

He grinned. "Only the beginning."

Chapter Twenty-Five

"We have about an hour and a half until we make the docks," Rory said, stroking Ginny's forehead until she awakened. She'd slept most of the way in the carriage, curled up on the seat next to him, her head on a pillow in his lap. "We could stop at an inn, if you'd like to sleep more comfortably until sunrise."

"Which is about what, an hour and a half away?" She grinned without opening her eyes.

"Yes, my little minx." He chuckled.

"Then wake me when we get to the dock. Once we're inside the cabin, I'm going to sleep all the way back to the States."

Rory leant down and kissed her temple. "I don't think you will be able to sleep. I have plans for you."

She didn't open her eyes, but she grinned.

* * * *

"A fine morning for a stroll, wouldn't you say, Miss Clark?" Rory had come through the doors of their state room out onto their private balcony, clad in his drawers.

Virginia grinned from beneath the wide-brimmed straw hat she used to cover her face as she reclined on a lounge chair, naked in the sun. He'd asked her that question on the voyage over under significantly different circumstances. They were the top balcony on the starboard side of the ship and no other passengers had taken up residence on either side of them. This luxury removed any qualms she'd normally have about letting the sun warm her skin in this provocative way. She was Rory's lover and Apollo's captive. What an utterly delicious fantasy.

Virginia could see just the outline of his beautiful body through the tiny holes of her hat as he gazed down at her. "In case you hadn't noticed, I lack the fabric, not to mention I can't walk." She felt his hand stroke down her thigh. His touch evoked a shiver that sent her nipples to pucker.

"And this is my fault?"

"Every single last bit of it."

"Even though it was you who vowed to reward me for every good deed I did since the beginning of summer all the way back to the States?"

"It was you who held me to that vow," she reminded him from underneath her hat.

He chuckled and she felt his weight settle at the foot of her chair. "How long have you been out here in the sun?" He lifted her right leg, bending it at the knee, and set her foot down to the right of the lounge chair.

"Oh, I don't know. Fifteen minutes at least. What are you doing?" she asked when her left foot touched the ground.

"I just don't want you to get sun-burned," he said just before his tongue slipped between her pussy lips.

"And this will help me stay shaded?" she moaned.

"Mmm-hmm."

His mouth was oddly cool as he suckled and licked her sun-warmed flesh. Her hips undulated and he expertly followed her every move, teasing, tickling, pleasuring.

"My God, you are hot. I have to get inside you." He removed her hat and pulled her up by her hands to a seated position.

Her chuckle echoed seductively. "I was hoping I'd entice you to another round."

With a growl he swept her up into his arms and once they'd crossed the threshold he tossed her onto the bed. Shucking his drawers, he crawled after her and drew in close. He grazed his fingers over her ribcage, feather light, purposefully avoiding her pebbled nipples. He lowered his face to her belly inhaling her scent all the way to her neck. "You are amazing. I am going to fuck you until the sun sets."

Her cunt clenched in anticipation of his promise. He sank his cock into her ever so slowly. She held her breath in order to fully experience each and every thick inch.

His body came to rest atop hers, his flesh cool against her heat. Buried to the hilt he gazed at her so affectionately, she could have cried. "I love you, you know."

Virginia felt her smile just about split her face in two. "I love you, too." Then she added brazenly, "Now get to it. And Rory?"

"Yes?"

"Hard."

"Yes, ma'am."

Virginia gripped his shoulders as he rammed into her. Her orgasm rocked her, body, mind and soul, and he was relentless. It didn't matter how many positions he'd switched to, on her side, legs in the air, up against the wall, on her hands and knees, hanging off the edge of the bed, she was sure she'd been coming the entire time he'd been fucking her, which had to have been for over an hour. Rory knew exactly how to handle her. He was an expert with her body. A virtuoso of carnal delights. One minute her muscles were straining as she came. Then, as if time hung suspended and the earth ceased to turn, there he was, stroking away her pain, coaxing her towards yet another chain of lush orgasmic waves, his slick skin sliding along hers, every nerve in her body alive with sensation.

Afterwards, as they lay in each other's arms engulfed in the afterglow, their conversation continued.

"How are you? I'm afraid I was none too gentle."

She giggled, leaned on her elbow and faced him. "Especially that last half."

"But you are all right, then? I didn't hurt you?"

There was no other way of putting it. She trailed a finger down his cheek. "Your love making is always perfect, regardless of how tender or rough. So I shall respond as follows—I am utterly sated." Then she added, as she plunged her gaze into his fathomless blue eyes, "And terribly in love."

He returned her hot look causing her stomach to flutter. "Can I assume that because you love me, you'll also marry me?"

Odd, but he'd finally offered for her and she felt something was not right. Her future was still up in the air; she at least needed to know in what direction she would go. She leaned up onto her elbow and looked into his eyes. "Once I know what my plans are I can more easily answer that question."

"Plans?"

"Of course. I didn't work all summer long as a chef only to get married and have children. That's not to say I don't want children...just not yet."

Thankfully, he didn't jump out of bed and storm out of the cabin as she imagined he might. "How long do you think it will be until you know for certain?"

"Honestly, I have no idea. What's out there for me, what possibilities may present themselves. I'm not even sure how to go about choosing."

He nodded once. "All right. I'll help you find your destiny," he vowed, his gaze dark with concern.

"Oh, Rory, I..."

"My father will be retiring soon. Ace and I will be taking over the running of the plantation for him in Virginia."

Virginia's spirit seemed to deflate. She knew, by simple mathematics, that this would decrease her options by drastic measures, unless of course, she and Rory's paths weren't meant to entwine. That thought alone left a cold lump of souring dough in her stomach.

The ominous cloud she'd felt looming in the distance settled itself over her dreams, threatening a damp and dreary future.

A future that just might be without Rory Hughson.

* * * *

Beatrice hadn't changed a thing in Virginia's old room—it was exactly as she had left it all those years ago before she left for school in New York. The upstairs maid had just unpacked the last of Virginia's

205

things and quit the room. Virginia fiddled with her certificate from the pastry contest, trying to smooth out a few creases courtesy of her trunk's contents.

A knock sounded at the door to her bedroom. "Come in."

A beaming Beatrice poked her head in. "Are you too tired for a visitor?"

"Beatrice!" Virginia set her certificate aside, jumped up from the bench at the foot of the bed and flew into the arms of her former guardian.

"Ginny, darling." The hug could have squeezed the breath from her had Virginia not been giving back the same. "The fabrics and trim you sent are simply stunning. I can't wait until we can visit the tailors together."

"I'm so glad you liked them. How was your ladies' society fundraiser tea?"

"Oh, that," Beatrice waved a hand in dismissal. "The tea raised an unprecedented amount of money, but I have to be honest with you. I don't wish to talk about the tea," she said. Her voice dropped to a more dire tone. "I've come for a different purpose altogether."

Virginia felt panic rise in her throat. "Is there something wrong? Is Luke all right?"

"Come, sit with me." Once they were comfortable upon the chocolate-coloured brocade fainting couch, Beatrice took Virginia by the hands. "Rory wrote to me shortly after you two arrived in France." She eyed Virginia. "By the sparkle in your eye and the rosy hue in your cheeks it seems you and Rory have…enriched your association since then."

Feeling scolded, Virginia removed her hands from Beatrice's and tried to fold a casual laugh into the mix. "Well, anyone would come to know each other better after spending an entire summer together."

Without batting an eye, Beatrice drove her point home. "I think you know what I mean."

Her mind raced. That was it. She'd been found out. Just like that. No pomp, no stolen diary page, not that she'd kept a diary. Beatrice knew her better than anyone, even more then her own mother. And now was she to be banished to the streets upon her arrival home for her lack of discretion with Mr Hughson the younger?

No. Impossible. Ginny couldn't find the words in her own defence nor concoct a lie. She respected Beatrice and would do so no matter the outcome.

With a shrug Beatrice added, "In company with this observation, I met Rory on the stairs a few minutes ago. He grabbed me by the shoulders and kissed both my cheeks." A sedate smile curved Beatrice's lips. "Even with all his flirting, he's never done such."

Virginia swallowed. "Does Luke know?"

"Not yet."

Virginia fell to her knees before Beatrice. "You can't let him in on my secret! He'll kill Rory!"

Beatrice chuckled. "First he'll kill him, then he'll make him marry you."

At once Virginia sobered, rose and sat beside Beatrice. "Actually, we've already discussed marriage."

A frown Virginia hadn't seen on Beatrice's face since the carriage incident settled on her features and her hands fisted in her lap. She was mad, not just regular mad, rattlesnake mad. "Did he turn you down?"

"No, no." Virginia shook her head. "In point of fact, it was I who turned him down."

Beatrice's eyes widened, her frown wiped away by a non-existent breeze. "What?"

As much as she wanted to gloss over the circumstances, Virginia felt that Beatrice should know the whole truth. "This past summer was the best of my life. I've been validated not only as a person, but my abilities as a chef." She smiled. "Not long after I arrived at Monsieur Leroux's château, I was named Head Chef. The next thing I knew, I was named winner over all the others who'd placed in a pastry contest, made up entirely out of male French pastry chefs. I'd certainly never brag, but these last three months have carved out a path to my future. I can't just drop everything and get married. This entire venture will have happened for naught."

Beatrice, who seemed to have been listening with the utmost patience, merely nodded. "Your argument is sound, my dear, and you have my promise that I won't let on to Luke about you and Rory. But I will warn you, if Luke finds out on his own, there won't be anything either of us can do about it."

"Of course." Relieved, Virginia hugged Beatrice. "Thank you so much. Your respect means the world to me, you know that?"

A dainty sniff came from Beatrice, but Virginia pretended not to hear. They recovered and grinned at each other, Virginia's secret stored deep inside, for now, anyway. "I have a bit of news for you that will likely brighten your day." Beatrice pulled a letter from her pocket and handed it to Virginia.

While Virginia read her letter, Beatrice paced back and forth in the room.

Virginia rose, folded the letter and tucked it into a drawer. She turned to Beatrice. "The Union Oyster House in Boston," Virginia said in awe, "wants me for their chef."

"They do." Beatrice's smile beamed. "Long ago, Luke visited the restaurant. He and the owner became acquainted over a few hands of cards, and since then have corresponded once or twice yearly. Luke mentioned you in his last letter and as it turned out, the Union Oyster House is in need of a chef."

"I'm so...so... I don't even know what I am." Virginia stared off across the room, not looking at anything in particular. "One of the oldest restaurants in Boston. Hm. Boston," she murmured. *So very far from Virginia.*

"Shall we expect an announcement regarding your new employment tonight? We're having a special welcome-home supper and Kane Hughson will be joining us."

Slowly, Virginia's attention came back to the conversation. "Kane. Rory and Luke's father?"

"Yes."

Virginia's hands suddenly became damp with moisture. "Beatrice, I'm going to need some time to think about the Union Oyster House's offer. If it's all right with you."

"Absolutely. But don't take too long or they'll get someone else."

She nodded, wishing things weren't so complicated.

"Will you join me in the kitchen later? Cook has been asking about you ever since this morning. He wants your opinion on the menu for tonight."

"Of course."

Beatrice gave Virginia one more hug and left the room.

Which will I give up, Head Chef at one of the oldest and most prestigious restaurants in Boston, or the love of my life? She buried her face in her hands and wept.

Chapter Twenty-Six

There was no way around it. Ace was about to find him out. Three months ago, he'd made it crystal-clear to his brother that he wasn't interested in Ginny romantically, but Rory had forgotten that Ace could read when a person was bluffing just by looking at him. His only salvation now was if Ace was out of practice. Rory and Luke now sat in the library waiting for their father to arrive for supper. He'd never bandied words with his elder brother over brandy before, but somehow they'd leapt into it as if they'd shared the tradition for years.

"Does Beatrice think Ginny and I are lovers?"

"Not that I'm aware. And perhaps it's better that way." Without pause, Ace continued his interrogation. "So I have your word that you and Virginia didn't cross that line at any time during the holiday?"

Rory nodded. "All I did for the entire summer was clean game hens." And honestly, Ace didn't have to know that he and Virginia had exercised their consent as adults and had fallen into each other's arms again. It wasn't his business, after all.

"You, cleaned game hens? Now this I don't believe."

"What, you think me incapable?"

"Not at all. It's just I've never seen you do a day's work in your life."

"I think I should resent that accusation, Ace. I'm the one who stayed here in Virginia whilst you roamed around playing cards with every Tom, Dick and Harry that could sit upright."

"Damn right. And I made a lot of money, too."

"And got into more trouble than you're worth."

Beatrice swept into the room where the love of her life and his younger brother were enjoying a tête-à-tête. Their voices hadn't noticeably risen, as far as she could ascertain, so she figured that it was safe to assume that Luke was yet unaware of his brother's liaison with Ginny. *And thank heavens for that.* She'd enough on her hands with the Hughson men the first time Rory and Ginny's amour had been revealed all those years ago. "Gentlemen, your father's carriage just pulled up to the front walk."

They stood.

"Now both of you behave yourselves." Beatrice brushed non-existent lint from their jackets with smart smacks to the fabric that translated all the way through to their skin.

"Ouch, Peaches. Easy now. Save your rough play for later tonight."

Rory choked.

"Luke," Beatrice reprimanded. "I'm going to have enough on my hands this evening without you and your innuendos."

"Innuendo? I thought I'd spoken quite plainly."

The butler entered. "Sir, Madam. Mr Kane Hughson."

Kane Hughson, the biggest, most robust older man Beatrice had ever met, strode around the butler as if he were a stone in the road.

"Ah, my beautiful daughter-in-law." He held his arms out to Beatrice who stepped readily into his embrace. He lifted her off the floor and moaned as he hugged her. "You smell good, you feel good... What are you doing here with these two boot-lickers? Run away with me to the old country."

His Irish accent coupled with his flirtations could make a woman forget who she was, but spotting Luke's glare at his sire's back, she didn't react. "Hello, Kane, it's lovely to see you, too. Now, put me down and go greet your boys."

"Last I heard you hated the old country," Luke said and received his father's crushing embrace.

"How can you hate anything with this comely lass by your side?" He indicated Beatrice and hugged Rory in the same fashion.

"Father," Rory acknowledged after he'd been set down.

"Mr Hughson," Virginia said from the door. "It's been so long," she added with the utmost grace from the doorway. She glided to him in the centre of the room and held out her hand to him. Beatrice felt pride for her as if it were her own daughter greeting the patriarch of the Hughson family like a queen.

"Mother Mary," Kane murmured. "Is this little Ginny all grown up, then?" He took her hand and placed a lingering kiss on the back. "I may never leave this house again. The view indoors is better than anything outside these walls."

"Kane," Luke interrupted. "Before you go spouting sonnets, would you like a brandy?"

Kane smiled at Virginia. "A good Irishman never resists a warm snifter and a beautiful woman. Or is that a warm woman and a beautiful snifter?"

"The former, I'm afraid," Rory said drolly. "However, in this case the brandy is the only thing up for consumption. The women are not."

Just after the men finished their brandies, the dinner bell rang. Kane escorted both Beatrice and Virginia into the dining room while Luke and Rory followed helplessly. It made Virginia smile the way they pretended to be jealous of their father. It was a funny sort of unspoken humour the all shared. How lucky for Rory to be part of such a loving family.

While the first course was served, Beatrice played hostess so perfectly that Virginia could only wish she had such poise.

"Tonight's menu is very special. Cook consulted with our own Chef Clark about the meal." Beatrice smiled at Virginia. "I'm so very proud of you, Ginny. We all are."

"Hear, hear." Luke raised his glass and everyone followed suit.

Kane cleared his throat. "Tell me about your French adventure, Ginny. Luke mentioned you'd won a contest at school and that's how you got the job."

"That is correct. The final judge, Monsieur Leroux, fell in love with my sweet cheese pastries and I was hired for the summer at his château just outside of Barbizon."

"And will we have the privilege of tasting your prize-winning delights any time soon?"

Virginia's cheeks heated to a nice simmer. "Mr Hughson, I will make them for you whenever you'd like."

"Grand," he grinned. "I've developed quite a sweet tooth in my autumn years."

Rory chuckled, but Luke laughed out loud. "Autumn? You mean winter, don't you?"

"Ha," Kane grunted. "A lot you know. Just because there's snow…"

Beatrice jumped in. "I see no snow on your roof, Kane. Only a few silver threads near your temples. A sure sign of wisdom."

"A sure sign of the graveyard," Rory teased.

"You're witness to the abuse my own sons dole out to me, Ginny. I receive more love from the Hughson women then I do the men, always have."

"Don't you worry about it." Virginia winked. "They'll get their share of snow one of these days."

"They will, but I promise you, neither of them will be as virile as I am." Kane struck himself in the chest with his fist.

The boys groaned and Beatrice glanced at Virginia trying to quell a grin.

"So back to this sweet tooth you've grown." Rory teased. "If you really want to satisfy this new impulse, you should try Virginia's latest creation, the wedding cake. With this she won sweepstakes at a French pastry contest, populated entirely with uppity French chefs."

"Did you now?" He grinned. Admiration shone in his mirthful gaze.

Virginia shot a brief, adoring look at Rory. "I did. But they weren't uppity, they were very gracious."

"To your face, but I'm sure they grumbled behind your back. They don't much like Americans over there."

Beatrice jumped in before Virginia could comment. "Rory, stop tormenting Ginny, she won and that's the main thing."

"It's all right, Beatrice. He's allowed his observations. I wouldn't have won without him, after all."

An odd sort of silence settled upon the room.

Kane leaned toward Virginia from across the table. "Without whom?"

"Without Rory." Beatrice's foot touched Virginia's under the table, the slight action sending red flags before her mind's eye.

"Rory went to France for this competition?"

Luke cleared his throat. "Rory pointed out that Virginia needed a chaperone and... Beatrice and I agreed that he should take on the position."

"You mean to say that you condoned this escapade?" Kane's voice boomed, causing the room to seem much smaller than it really was.

After a brief glance ricocheted from Luke to Beatrice to Virginia to Rory. Nary a comment was uttered between the four of them and Virginia felt herself sinking into her chair.

"Are you daft? You can't let a randy youth run wild with a beautiful woman in France! All sorts of untoward things can occur."

"Don't worry. I have Rory's word that nothing improper happened." Luke's gaze landed on Rory. "*Don't I, Rory?*"

Virginia watched as Luke eyed his petrified brother for what seemed an overly-long amount of time.

The youngest Hughson swallowed audibly.

Luke looked as if he could skin his brother alive. "Rory, you *swore...*"

"Have you gone and hit your head, man? Of course he did!" Instantly, Kane's regard landed slap on Virginia. His gaze softened some, but he didn't say a word.

From across the table, Rory stood. "I realise that this is the most unromantic proposal ever uttered, but... Virginia, will you marry me?"

She didn't have to think about her answer. "Yes."

"Ginny dear, what about the Union Oyster House in Boston?"

Following Beatrice's question, Rory eyed Virginia. "What about the Union Oyster house in Boston?"

Virginia felt herself wince. "They've asked me to be their head chef."

Kane folded his arms across his chest. "They can bloody well shuck their own oysters. Rory will open a restaurant for you right here."

Virginia watched Rory to gauge his response.

He strode around the table to her side. "The idea isn't all that far-fetched."

"And you would be all right with me working every day?"

Rory held out a hand and pulled her to her feet. "Tuesday through Saturday, lunch and supper only."

Virginia closed the minimal distance between then and slid her arms up his chest to entwine around his neck. "You have yourself a deal."

"I have myself a wife," he murmured and bent his head to hers for a kiss, however, Kane cleared his throat.

The heat of a blush suffused Virginia's cheeks and she stepped out of his arms.

"We'd better make this a fast one," Luke said, thoroughly amused.

Beatrice wadded up her linen napkin and tossed it at her husband. "Like ours was?"

Kane chuckled. "Hot Irish blood is both a blessing and a curse."

Rory slipped his arm around Virginia and pulled her close. "Thank God for that. Clark is Irish, isn't it?"

She smiled. "Did you even have to ask?"

About the Author

Born and reared in Southern California, Genella deGrey longed to be your typical blonde, tanned, surfer girl but failed miserably. Unable to sit idle without falling asleep, she embarked upon several artistic endeavours. Make-up and set dressing for the entertainment industry, Resort Enhancement for The Walt Disney Company and writing sexy historical romance top the list of her favourite activities. A consummate closet goth and amateur music and (red) wine enthusiast, she is also a hopeless romantic awaiting the arrival of her very own Mr Romance/Soul Mate with whom to share the rest of her life.

Genella deGrey loves to hear from readers. You can find her contact information, website details and author profile page at http://www.total-e-bound.com.

Total-E-Bound Publishing

www.total-e-bound.com

Take a look at our exciting range of literagasmic™
erotic romance titles and discover pure quality
at Total-E-Bound.